Teddy Jo
and the
Terrible
Secret

Teddy Jo

and the terrible secret

HILDA STAHL

Tyndale House
Publishers, Inc.
Wheaton, Illinois

Dedicated with love to
Eldon, Kay, Tera, Jeanna, Ryan
and Brandon Willard

First printing, September 1982

Library of Congress Catalog Card Number 82-60013
ISBN 0-8423-6943-0, paper
Copyright © 1982 by Hilda Stahl
Printed in the United States of America

contents

1

Terrible News

Teddy Jo hooked her thumb in the hole of her short cotton nighty as she slowly crept from the bathroom. She twisted and twisted until the nighty was wrapped around her hand and hugged tightly against her thin body. She licked her dry lips as she stared at the half-open bedroom door just on the other side of the door to her room. Maybe she should scream and scream and say that she'd had a bad nightmare. Maybe then they'd stop fighting.

Her stomach tightened and a bitter taste filled her mouth. She should slip back into bed beside Linda and cover her head with a pillow. She shivered, then tiptoed toward the half-open door. A light spread across the worn carpet of the hall. She stopped just outside the light against the wall, one hand wrapped with her nighty, the other clutching at her dry throat.

"I've got to have room to breathe, Carol!"

Her dad's voice was sharp and Teddy Jo wanted to run back to her room, but she stayed very still.

"How much room do you need, Larry? Does it take more space than this?"

Larry was quiet a long time and Teddy Jo carefully peeked around the door. Mom sat on the bed with her knees up under her chin and Dad stood near the dresser, a tired look on his face.

"I'm leaving, Carol."

Teddy Jo bit back a gasp as she jerked out of sight. Was Dad serious? Would he really leave this time?

"Maybe I'll be back the end of summer. Maybe I won't."

"And who are you taking?" snapped Carol. "Paul? Linda? Teddy Jo?"

"Use what little brains you have, Carol! I can't take any of them. How would I manage?"

"And how am *I* supposed to manage? I have a job! The kids are too little to stay by themselves!"

Tears burned Teddy Jo's eyes and she blinked hard. She would not cry! Mom and Dad always fought and Dad never left.

"I am going, Carol. And I'm going alone. I need to find a job. My unemployment has almost run out and that little bit you get from Jacob's is peanuts."

"At least it feeds us! It keeps this roof over our head!"

Teddy Jo looked up at the ceiling and barely made out the water spot in the shape of Michigan. She knew the spot where they lived. Someday she'd drag a chair over and mark it with a red magic marker.

But maybe she wouldn't be living here if Dad left. Mom would have to find a smaller and a cheaper place. If there was such a place.

"Put those clothes back, Larry! You can't leave us! What would we do?" The bed springs creaked.

"I'm going, Carol. You can't stop me this time."

"Then you are going to take Teddy Jo!"

"No way! I won't take that little pistol!"

Teddy Jo pressed a trembling hand to her mouth. Her stomach felt like a tight hard ball of ice.

"What will I do with her? I can't handle her."

"I can't either. Where's that other brown sock?"

"Who cares about a brown sock? I'm talking about that ten-year-old daughter of yours."

A dresser drawer slammed. "*Your* daughter. I won't take any blame for the way she is."

Teddy Jo pressed against the wall. What did he mean? She was no worse than Paul or Linda.

Carol sighed loudly. "I could send her to Dad."

Larry chuckled. "It would serve the old man right."

"Maybe we could all go stay with Dad awhile."

"No! I won't stay with that man! He's strange. He hasn't been right for years and you know it."

Teddy Jo clamped her teeth tightly and frowned. They would not make her live with old weird Grandpa! No way!

"Maybe he'd loan us money just until you found a job."

"Don't you dare ask him! I won't live off him. Do you hear me? If you and the kids want to, that's your business. I'm going to Flint and hunt for a job. Maybe Detroit."

"Larry. Larry. There are jobs in Grand Rapids. We could look there and we'd be close to Dad and he could help us with the kids even if we didn't borrow money from him."

"Do you think I want to live in Middle Lake again? We left there twelve years ago and I'm not going back!"

"What will I tell the kids? You can't just walk out now in the middle of the night!"

"I'm going."

Teddy Jo dashed to her room, her heart racing painfully. She slipped under the sheet and huddled close to Linda's back.

Finally her heart stopped hammering in her ears. She heard Linda's gentle breathing and then a door slammed.

Dad was gone.

She clenched her fists and anger rose inside her. She yanked on the top sheet, then kicked Linda hard. "Get over, will you? Do you have to hog the whole bed?"

Linda jerked up with a scream. "What's wrong with you, you little demon? You are the worst little sister in the entire world!"

Teddy Jo wanted to throw something through the window. "I didn't ask to share a room or a bed with you, did I? Go sleep with Paulie. He's too little to care if he has to share."

Just then Mom rushed into the room and flicked the light on. She stood in her knee-length pink nightgown and her dark hair covered her slender shoulders and hung down her back. "What's going on this time? I thought you girls were asleep."

"Teddy Jo kicked me!" cried Linda, glaring at Teddy Jo.

"She took my share of the bed!" Teddy Jo doubled her fists and stood on the floor near her side of the bed. "How can I sleep with her shoving me out on the floor?"

Carol pushed her hair back with trembling hands. "Girls, just get into bed. I'm too tired for this."

Linda sighed and slipped into bed, pulling the sheet over her thin body. "Good night, Mom."

"Good night, Linda. Stay on your side of the

bed." She looked at Teddy Jo with a tired sigh. "Go to bed, Teddy Jo. I don't want any more trouble."

"Why don't you send Dad in to settle it?" Teddy Jo waited, barely breathing.

"He's asleep. Now get to bed."

Teddy Jo turned her face away before Mom saw the burning tears as she slid into bed. What would Mom say to them tomorrow? Would she tell them that Dad had gone away on business?

Carol snapped off the light and Teddy Jo stared into the darkened room. Tears slipped from the corners of her eyes down into her ears and her dark hair. She lay very still with her small fists doubled at her sides and her heart almost exploding inside her thin chest.

Nobody wanted her. Not Dad or Mom or Linda, and probably not even their weird grandpa who lived at Middle Lake.

She heard something strange and she carefully lifted her head, frowning slightly as she listened. Someone was crying hard and Teddy Jo knew it was Mom.

Teddy Jo flipped onto her side and fiercely jabbed her pillow, then dropped her head on it, drawing her bony knees to her chin. She closed her eyes tightly and pressed her hand over the ear that wasn't buried in her pillow.

If she was lucky, tomorrow would never come.

2
The Long Trip

Teddy Jo clasped the box of Cheerios to her thin chest as she stared at Mom and Linda.

"I'm not going to Grandpa's!" cried Linda, stamping her foot. "I'll run away! I'll kill myself!"

Carol grabbed Linda's arms and shook her until her hair flipped back and forth. "You will do as I say! Dad is gone for a while and we can't pay the rent here for another month. We are leaving today!"

Linda jerked away and her blue eyes were bright with unshed tears. She glared at Carol. "I'll call Sharon Franklin and stay with her. Her parents won't mind. I can't leave here now."

Carol pushed the newspaper off the kitchen chair and sat down. "What will Sharon's family think if you stay with them? You're twelve years old, Linda. You just can't stay

13

here with Sharon while we drive across the state to live."

Teddy Jo eased herself down onto a chair and wondered how Paul could hear the cartoons on TV over the loud voices of Mom and Linda. Maybe Paul had learned to shut out the fighting.

Linda tugged her tee shirt over her denim shorts. Her blue eyes were wide and pleading. "Mom, they want me to stay with Sharon. She doesn't have a sister and we've been best friends for the three years that we've lived here. Please, Mom. You can get settled at Grandpa's and then get me later. Please."

Carol rubbed her bare arms and sighed. "If Sharon's parents agree, then you can stay."

Linda leaped up with a wide smile. "Thanks, Mom. I'll call her this minute and find out."

Teddy Jo watched Linda run to the phone in the living room, then slowly set the box of Cheerios on the table. She wasn't really hungry this morning. She looked at Mom through narrowed eyes. "I'm not going to Grandpa's either."

Carol shoved her chair back and jumped up. "Oh, yes you are! I won't even discuss it! You are going to pack this minute!"

Teddy Jo grabbed the sugar bowl and pulled her arm back, but before she could throw it, Carol grabbed her arm and wrenched the bowl away, spilling sugar on the table and the floor and Teddy Jo's left foot.

14

"You will not cause any trouble, Theodora Josephine! You will help me get our things together so we can get out of here." Carol gripped Teddy Jo so tightly that she cried out in pain.

"I want Dad. I want him right now!"

"Well, he's not here." Carol stepped away from Teddy Jo. "I want my dad, too. And I want him right now." Her voice sounded full of tears and Teddy Jo wanted to put her arms around Mom and hug her tightly, but she couldn't.

Carol sagged against the counter near the sink, her head down. She was dressed in blue shorts and a white knit shirt with a scoop neck. "How could my life turn out this way? Is there any hope?"

Teddy Jo bit her bottom lip and blinked hard to keep the tears back. Mom was grown up. How could she feel that way? She didn't have anyone pushing her around and telling her what to do. Nobody was making her go stay with Grandpa.

Several hours later Teddy Jo sat in the corner of the back seat of the old brown Chevy and watched the houses and the mailboxes and the cars. Loud music from the radio boomed over her head and around her ears and she wanted to shout at Mom to turn it down.

Paul sat in his corner, his eyes glued to a comic book.

Mom had said that they'd be at Grandpa's

house in two-and-a-half hours. She'd told Linda that she would come pick her up in three weeks no matter what. Linda had shrugged, then run away with Sharon Franklin to find boys to talk to.

Teddy Jo wrinkled her small nose. She'd never go crazy over boys the way Linda did.

Where was Dad now? Would he really stay away for the summer? Or maybe forever?

Teddy Jo groaned and pulled her knees up to her chin and wrapped her arms around her legs. She wouldn't think about Dad. So what if he didn't come back to them? He never paid any attention to her anyway except to say, "Will you be quiet, Teddy Jo? I can't hear the TV while you're running your mouth."

Just then Paul squirmed in his seat. "I gotta go to the bathroom, Mom. I can't wait!"

Teddy Jo frowned. Why did he always wait until the last minute?

Carol frowned into the rearview mirror. "I'll stop as soon as I can. I told you not to drink so much soda the last time we stopped."

"I only had a can of Vernors."

"One can too many," muttered Teddy Jo as Mom pulled off the highway at a rest stop. Maybe if Paul worked it just right they'd never get to Grandpa's.

The sun was low in the sky by the time Carol drove through Middle Lake, then turned onto a dirt road. Teddy Jo's heart beat faster and the neck of her tee shirt felt as if it was choking her.

Carol switched off the radio and the only sound was a fly buzzing at the window near Paul.

"I walked down this road lots of times," said Carol in a light voice. "See those trees, kids? I played there. It seems like yesterday. It seems like a million years ago."

Teddy Jo heard the catch in Mom's voice. A dog ran alongside the car, barking at the tires.

"You'll hit it, Mom!" cried Paul, his face white as he pressed his nose against the window. "Be careful!"

"That dog doesn't worry me at all." Carol slowed and turned into a short drive and the dog ran back to his home. Carol stopped the car outside a small garage, then looked back at Teddy Jo and Paul. "We're here." She looked relieved but she didn't smile.

Teddy Jo swallowed hard and looked at the old white house and the small lawn and all the trees. She caught her breath as a tall, broad man with gray hair walked toward the car.

Was that her weird grandpa?

3

Grandpa Korman

Even though it was hot, Teddy Jo shivered as she stood behind Mom. Paul stepped close to Teddy Jo until he was touching her and she wanted to put her arms around him and tell him that everything would be all right. But she knew it wouldn't be.

"This is your Grandpa Korman, kids," said Carol brightly as she turned around to them. "Teddy Jo, Paul, say hello to your grandpa."

Grandpa looked as big as one of the trees in the front yard. He was dressed in loose-fitting tan pants and a short-sleeved shirt that matched. He held his big hand out to Paul. "I'm glad to meet you, Paul. I guess I forgot you could be this big. I was expecting to see a baby." Grandpa chuckled and Paul finally held out his hand.

Teddy Jo stepped back and folded her arms across her thin chest and stared at the big

19

stranger. If he tried to shake hands with her, she'd bite him.

"Hello, Teddy Jo." Grandpa smiled at her and she noticed that one front tooth had a small chip missing. He pushed his hands into his pockets and jingled change and keys. "You get prettier every time I see you."

Teddy Jo's blue eyes widened. Did he really think she was pretty? Nobody had ever said so before. They always said Linda was.

"You were three years old the last time I saw you." Grandpa nodded. "I'm glad to see you again."

"I'll get our things out of the car, Dad," Carol said stiffly. "I don't like to put you out, but we had nowhere to go."

Grandpa patted Carol's shoulder. "You are always welcome here. This is your home and it always will be."

Carol scowled and walked to the back of the car.

Teddy Jo looked around at the yard and tried to imagine Mom as a little girl playing here, but she couldn't.

A dog barked from across the road and Teddy Jo saw a boy about her age playing in front of the small house with a small black dog. Just then the boy looked her way and saw her watching him. He waved and she quickly turned away. She wasn't going to wave at any strange boy.

"Help me carry, Teddy Jo." Mom pushed a

20

small box into Teddy Jo's arms. "Those are your clothes and I want you to keep track of them yourself."

"I'll show you your rooms," said Grandpa, leading the way with his arms full. He walked up the two steps and opened the door to the front porch. He stepped aside and finally Teddy Jo with Paul close behind walked in. The door into the house was wide open and the smell of fried chicken filled the air. Teddy Jo's stomach tightened with hunger and that made her mad. She didn't want to eat anything that Grandpa cooked.

Grandpa walked through the front room, then up a flight of narrow wooden stairs. Teddy Jo walked behind him, and Paul behind her. She could hear Mom behind Paul.

"There are two rooms up here," said Grandpa. "The kids will sleep in here where we have twin beds, and Carol, you sleep in the other."

Teddy Jo opened her mouth to say she wasn't sharing a room with Paul because he always wet the bed and made the place smell terrible, but she saw the strained look on his pale face and she snapped her mouth closed tightly. She set her box of clothes on the bed closest to the window and heard Grandpa and Mom talking in the room across from them, but she didn't listen to what they were saying. Teddy Jo slowly looked around. At least it was clean and it was not as tiny as the

21

room she'd shared with Linda. The light green walls and dark green curtains were very pretty.

"I don't want to stay here," whispered Paul, leaning against Teddy Jo and looking up into her face. "I want to go home. I want Dad."

Tears stung her eyes and she pushed Paul away. There was no way she was going to cry in front of Paul and where Mom and Grandpa could hear her. "You'll get used to it here. You'll probably even like it here."

Paul sniffed hard and rubbed his fist across his eyes. "I gotta go to the bathroom. Where's the bathroom?"

"Go ask Grandpa. It's his house."

Paul shook his head, his blue eyes wide. "I won't ask him! You ask him!"

"No way! I'm not talking to him." She rubbed her hands down her shorts, then grabbed Paul's arm. "Oh, come on. We'll find the bathroom. It's downstairs somewhere."

At the head of the stairs she stopped short as Grandpa said just behind her, "Supper's ready and I know you kids are hungry. I'll show you where you can wash up."

Teddy Jo stood blocking the way and she wanted to push past the others and run to her new room and stay away from everyone.

"Will you hurry, Teddy Jo!" said Carol sharply. "What're you waiting for? I want to eat. I need a cup of coffee."

Teddy Jo rushed down the steep stairs, her sandals clattering loudly. She almost bumped into a large rocker, then ran around it and stopped at the first open door. It was the bathroom. Paul rushed past her and slammed and locked the door.

"You can wash in the kitchen," said Carol as she walked through another door that led to a large kitchen.

Teddy Jo held her hands under the warm water as she looked over her shoulder at the round wooden table already set with four plates. This was the biggest kitchen she'd ever seen. It even had room for the clothes washer and dryer. Everything looked clean and tidy. She couldn't picture Grandpa with a dust rag in his large hands.

Carol picked up a large glass vase. "Oh, Dad," she whispered. "You still have it."

"Sure I do, honey. Momma and I loved that. You worked real hard to save money to buy that for us. It was Momma's favorite and she always took special care of it."

"I wish Momma was still alive." Carol carefully set the vase on the shelf next to the large window behind the table. "I need her now, Dad."

"Carol, that need you feel inside would still be there even if Momma was alive. That need is for God."

"Don't start, Dad!" Carol lifted her chin and her blue eyes snapped. "I don't want to hear that and you know it!"

Teddy Jo dried her hands slowly and

23

wondered why Mom didn't want to hear about God. What was so bad about God?

Paul walked slowly into the kitchen, then sidled up to Mom, his head down. His tee shirt was half in and half out of his brown shorts. A shoelace hung down his worn tennis shoe.

"Let's eat," said Grandpa as he set a platter of fried chicken on the table. He took a salad out of the refrigerator and a dish of mashed potatoes out of the oven where they'd kept warm.

Teddy Jo sat beside Paul and across from Grandpa. He smiled at her but she looked down at her plate with a frown. She wasn't going to get friendly with this big man. And if Paul did, she'd punch his lights out.

"Heavenly Father, thank you for my fine family," prayed Grandpa, and Teddy Jo looked up in surprise. Grandpa had his head bowed and his eyes closed. Carol did, too, but Paul was looking as surprised as Teddy Jo.

Finally Grandpa finished praying, then said, "Paul, do you want a drumstick?"

Paul nodded slightly and Grandpa laid a crispy brown drumstick on Paul's white plate.

"What about you, Teddy Jo?" Grandpa smiled at her with the platter in his big hand.

She just looked at him and he winked and laid a drumstick on her plate. She didn't mean to pick it up and eat it, but she was too hungry.

She also ate buttered corn, mashed potatoes, tossed salad, and two rolls.

"You're a good cook, Dad," said Carol in surprise.

"I enjoy cooking, and especially when I have someone to cook for." Grandpa picked up his glass and drank the rest of his water.

Teddy Jo sat back and looked at him and he winked at her again. A strange warmth spread over her and she locked her fingers together in her lap. She was not going to smile at him or say thank you for supper or anything.

4
Mark Allen

The next morning Teddy Jo opened her eyes and looked around in surprise. This wasn't her room and she wasn't sleeping next to Linda.

Teddy Jo sat bolt upright. She was at Grandpa's house. Paul slept in the bed across the room. His light blanket was dragging on the floor and just a corner of it covered Paul's thin body. He hadn't wet the bed.

Teddy Jo swung her bare legs off the bed and stood up, her cotton nighty brushing her knees. She might as well get dressed and look around outdoors. She'd never lived in the country before and it might be kind of fun to explore. Grandpa would never know. He was probably still asleep. She peeked out the window at the bright summer day, then pulled on the same clothes she had worn yesterday.

She carried her sandals so they wouldn't clatter on the steps.

The door to Grandpa's bedroom was closed as she tiptoed to the bathroom. She caught a glimpse of her reflection and wrinkled her nose. She should brush her hair. She shrugged. What did it matter? She hadn't brushed it yesterday either. Maybe tomorrow she'd get around to it. Linda brushed and combed her hair fifty times a day at least.

Teddy Jo sat on a wooden chair at the kitchen table and hooked her sandals in place. She frowned as her stomach growled. How could she be hungry after last night? Well, it was just too bad because she was not going to eat another meal that Grandpa cooked. He could wink at her and smile at her forever, but she still wouldn't like being here.

She walked toward the back door, then looked longingly at the refrigerator. She sighed, then jerked it open and looked inside. She could have a glass of milk. He hadn't cooked that. But he had bought it. She poured herself a glass of milk, then set the jug back in the refrigerator. Right next to it sat a plastic-wrapped plate of leftover fried chicken. She groaned, then pulled out a big piece of white meat and ate it along with gulps of cold milk.

Well, she sure wouldn't eat any lunch no matter what.

She opened the back door and it led immediately into the backyard. A warm gentle wind blew against her and it felt good. There were no fumes in the air or factory smoke or anything.

Fluffy white clouds dotted the bright blue sky. The clouds looked like big cotton balls that she could easily pluck from the sky, but she wasn't that dumb. She'd learned some science even if she'd failed the class.

The grass felt soft and springy under Teddy Jo's feet as she walked toward a small shed with a wire pen beside it. She stopped beside the pen and her eyes grew round and she said, "Oh!" She locked her hands tightly together in front of her. A small deer stood inside the pen with its large ears high and its big brown eyes watching her. Its back was covered with white spots and it had the tiniest hooves in the whole world.

"The little fawn lost her momma last month and I've been nursing her," said Grandpa softly from beside Teddy Jo.

"Is she a wild deer?"

"Yes. A whitetail. As soon as she can manage on her own, I'll set her free." He held a bucket with a large white nipple on it. "I'm going to feed her now. Would you like to do it?"

Teddy Jo nodded, then suddenly remembered that she wasn't speaking to this man.

"Feed it yourself. It's your deer."

"I don't mind sharing the pleasure," said Grandpa as he opened the small gate and stepped inside the pen. The fawn ran to him, butting against the bucket.

Teddy Jo wanted to turn and run back to the house, but she couldn't miss out on watching the fawn suck the nipple of the bucket. She'd never seen such a thing in her life, not even in a library book.

"I've taken care of several deer each year," said Grandpa as he held the bucket steady while the fawn sucked noisily. "I have a rabbit with a broken leg in the shed. He's mending and I'll turn him loose in a couple of weeks. Once I had a baby fox and two young raccoons."

Teddy Jo could hardly breathe. Was it possible to be this close to someone who loved animals and took care of them? She'd never had even a goldfish or a turtle for a pet. Once Paul had brought home a stray kitten, but Mom had made him get rid of it.

"Come on in here and pet the fawn," said Grandpa, holding the gate open.

She hesitated, then walked in and touched it. She jerked her hand back, her eyes wide in alarm.

"This little gal likes to have you stroke her," said Grandpa with a chuckle. He scratched the fawn's neck and it leaned against him.

Finally Teddy Jo touched the fawn again.

The hair was coarse and smelled dusty, but Teddy Jo wanted to keep petting it.

"We have company, Teddy Jo," said Grandpa with a laugh. "Hi ya, Mark. You're up bright and early on this Sunday morning."

"I wanted to see if you'd like to ride to church with us," Mark said, eyeing Teddy Jo as he talked to Grandpa.

Teddy Jo met him look for look and finally he looked away. His small black dog wriggled at his side.

"Not today, Mark, but thanks anyway." Grandpa held the gate open and motioned for Teddy Jo to walk out. She did, but she hated leaving the fawn. It followed her to the gate, then stood and looked at her.

"Mark Allen, this is Teddy Jo Miller, my granddaughter." Grandpa sounded very proud and Teddy Jo looked up at him in surprise. Was he proud of her or of Mark Allen?

"Hi, Teddy Jo," said Mark with a smile. He had brown curly hair and dark brown eyes. He had on blue dress levis and a short-sleeved white shirt that buttoned down the front. "Are you going to church with Grandpa this morning, Teddy Jo?"

She shot a look at Grandpa, but before she could say anything he said, "We didn't discuss it yet, Mark. Why don't you come over this afternoon and you and Teddy Jo will have more time to get acquainted."

"All right, and maybe we can play Monopoly," said Mark excitedly. But Teddy Jo muttered, "No way."

Mark said goodbye, then ran with his black dog around the house.

"He's a nice boy, Teddy Jo. You'll like him."

"I hate boys. Linda would like him, but he looks a little young for her."

Grandpa laughed and shook his gray head. "I didn't mean like him for a boyfriend. You have lots of years for that." He rinsed the bucket out at the outdoor faucet, then set it upside down in the grass. "Would you like to go to church and Sunday school with me? Your mother is going to stay home, but you and Paul can go with me if you want."

Teddy Jo tipped her head sideways and looked at Grandpa. So Mom wouldn't go. She probably didn't want to hear anything about God. "I think I'll go with you."

"Good. I'll like taking you. I get lonely sometimes with no family around me. Oh, I have friends, good friends, but that isn't family, is it?"

She hadn't thought about family before. Hers had always been pulling away from each other, fighting and arguing. She walked beside the big stranger who was her very own grandpa, her family, and she felt strange. Did she want him to be important to her the way he seemed to think she was important to him?

He stopped in the kitchen and looked down at her. "I'll help you brush your hair if you want."

She frowned and a flush started deep inside her. Did he think that she was such a baby that she couldn't brush her own hair? "You get yourself ready and I'll get myself ready."

He nodded. "That's a fair deal. And I'll try not to treat you like a baby if you treat me like your grandpa."

She stepped back, her eyes wide. "I sure won't climb on your lap and hug and kiss you!"

"I'd like some hugs and kisses from you, but I guess I can live without them. But I would like someone to take walks with and talk to and play Monopoly with."

She frowned and shook her head. "You can't like playing games with kids."

"I do."

She saw the sincere look in his eye and she knew he meant what he said. She twisted her toe. "If I'm here long enough I'll play games with you and I might go for walks with you. If I'm here long enough!"

He bent down and kissed her cheek and she jumped back with a yell, her hand where he'd kissed her. "You said you wouldn't kiss me, but I didn't say anything about not kissing you. You're my special Teddy Jo and I love you."

She ran from the kitchen and up the stairs, her heart racing. He had kissed her! No one—

not even Dad or Mom—had kissed her that she could remember.

She stood near the dresser and looked at her flushed face in the mirror. He'd said she was special and that he loved her.

Abruptly she turned from the mirror, tugging her shirt off over her head. How could he love her? He didn't know how mean she really was. Nobody loved her. Grandpa would find out soon enough.

5
Goodbye, Mom

Teddy Jo walked listlessly around a tall tree, then stopped and looked around. Everything seemed very familiar now. She and Paul had taken several walks with Grandpa around the farm and he'd told her about the acres and acres of black walnut trees that were so precious to him. She couldn't understand how anyone could feel that way about a tree, but if Grandpa wanted to, then he could, for all she cared.

She picked a leaf off a maple tree and stripped it. For four Sundays now she'd gone to Sunday school and church with Grandpa. Today she'd heard something that had surprised her. Peggy, the teacher, had stood in front of the class of boys and girls and Teddy Jo had sat right in her usual place beside Mark.

"Many boys and girls don't know that they are loved," Peggy had said. She had looked very pretty in her yellow dress, with yellow barrettes holding back her dark hair. Even her shoes were yellow. Teddy Jo had looked at Peggy and listened hard instead of squirming restlessly to get outdoors.

"God loves boys and girls," Peggy had said. "God loves you." And she'd looked right at Teddy Jo. "He does! He loves you just the way you are. He wants to be a Father as well as a God to you. He wants you to have a personal relationship with him. And you can, because Jesus made it possible by dying on the cross, then coming back to life to be in heaven forever."

Teddy Jo had heard some of this before and she hadn't paid much attention, but today it seemed to make sense to her. Grandpa had said often enough that each person had an empty spot inside that could only be filled with God.

Teddy Jo sighed and dropped the remains of the leaf on the ground. God really loved her! It didn't seem possible.

She walked to the pen and looked at the fawn. Grandpa had said just this morning that it was almost time to turn it loose. Teddy Jo groaned as she reached out and stroked the fawn's face.

"How can you let it go if you really love it?" Teddy Jo had asked as she'd looked up at Grandpa.

He had reached out to pat her shoulder, but she'd jumped back and his hand had fallen to his side. "Teddy Jo, I'll set the little gal free *because* I love her. She belongs out in the woods and on the hills. I want her to have a happy life with other deer."

Teddy Jo had walked to the house with tears in her eyes. She didn't want to see the fawn leave ever.

She looked at the fawn now and sighed again. A fly buzzed around it and it flicked its long white tail. Teddy Jo sniffed and turned toward the house. Later this afternoon Mark was coming over so they could finish their Monopoly game.

She looked across toward Mark's house as Chainsaw barked loudly. Mark always brought Chainsaw with him and Grandpa even let him in the house.

She tugged a ponytail that hung over her ear. Grandpa had said the July sun was too hot for her to have her long hair on her neck. He had brushed it and hooked it up with pony-tail bands he'd bought when he bought groceries.

Teddy Jo walked into the kitchen and could still smell the aroma of roast beef from Sunday dinner. The house seemed very quiet. She knew Grandpa was still taking his Sunday afternoon nap and that Mom was in her room upstairs. The TV was off so Paul was probably in their bedroom reading a comic. He didn't really read it. He looked at the pictures and tried to imagine what it said. He was too little to read every word.

Teddy Jo stood at the bottom of the steep stairs and looked up. A shiver ran up and down her spine and she frowned. Why did she suddenly feel as if something terrible was going to happen?

Someone walked across the floor upstairs and she knew it was Mom. Slowly Teddy Jo walked up, her hand on the plastered wall, her head up. She needed to be with someone right now and get rid of this scary feeling. Mom was up. She wouldn't get mad if she was disturbed right now.

Teddy Jo stopped outside Mom's open door. Mom stood beside the bed dressed in her new white slacks and peach colored knit shirt. Her dark hair hung down, almost blocking out her profile. A red suitcase lay open on the bed.

Teddy Jo's heart leaped. They were going home again! Dad must have called and said that he didn't really want to be without them, that he missed them a lot and wanted to be a family again.

Mom turned and nervously pushed her hair behind her ears. The sun streamed in through the window and made the room stuffy. "Hi, Teddy Jo. I thought you were out for a walk."

"Are we leaving, Mom?" Teddy Jo looked from the half-packed suitcase to Mom's face. Something in Mom's eyes made Teddy Jo's stomach tighten.

"I can't stay here forever, Teddy Jo. I called your dad today and he said maybe we could try again. He said he found a job. It's not in a factory and it doesn't pay much, but it's a job. And I can get a job and we can make ends meet. I have to pick Linda up from Sharon's house first thing tomorrow. I called her and told her to be ready."

"I'll pack my stuff. It won't take long. I'll help Paulie with his." Teddy Jo turned to leave, but Mom touched her arm and she turned back, her eyebrows raised questioningly.

"You're staying here, Teddy Jo." Mom's voice was very quiet, very determined.

Teddy Jo shook her head and her ponytails flipped. "No! No, I am not! I'm going with you. I am!"

Mom rubbed her slender hands together. Her long fingernails were painted a dull pink. A small diamond flashed on her left hand. "Teddy Jo, I can't take you. I'll get you when school starts. I promise. I just can't have you now for the rest of July and August. Linda will be able to watch Paul while I'm at work. If you were there we'd have to hire a baby-sitter and we can't afford it."

"I am going with you." She folded her arms in front of her and closed her mouth stubbornly.

"You are staying here! You're staying with Grandpa." Mom sounded very stern.

"You can't make me!" Teddy Jo stamped her foot hard. "You can't make me stay here with that weird old man!"

"Teddy Jo! You watch what you say! You like your grandpa! You've been getting along just fine with him." Mom twisted her fingers together and her cheeks flushed bright red. "I don't want you throwing any fit. I can't take it right now. I got a long drive ahead of me. For once in your life think of someone besides yourself."

Teddy Jo wanted to throw herself to the floor and kick and scream the way she'd done so many times before, but she knew Grandpa would come running and make her stop. "I'll go pack. I'll be ready and I'll get in the car and go with you." Her heart raced and a bitter taste filled her mouth. She couldn't stay here with Grandpa without Mom and Paul. How could she sleep in her room if Paul wasn't in the bed across from hers? She rushed to the room with Mom close behind her.

Paul sat on his bed, his face pale, a comic in his hands. The ammonia smell stung Teddy Jo's nose and she knew Paul had sat right there and wet the bed. He wouldn't look up even when she grabbed a box and started stuffing her clothes in it.

Mom grabbed Paul's arm and pulled him off the bed. "Get some clean clothes and get down to the bathroom and change! And you wash yourself. We're not going to drive all the way to Flint with you smelling that way."

Paul grabbed the first thing he found and ran out, his blue eyes wide and scared in his little pale face.

Teddy Jo wanted to run after him and tell him she'd take care of him, but she couldn't. She couldn't even take care of herself.

Mom yanked the box from Teddy Jo and held it away from her. "You are staying here, young lady, and I won't have any more fuss! Grandpa said he could handle you. Grandpa said he wouldn't have any problem with you."

Teddy Jo stood dead in her tracks and stared up at Mom. Grandpa had said he could *handle* her? Why hadn't he said that he loved her and wanted her? Maybe then she'd have stayed. "Give me that box, Mom! I won't stay in this rotten house another minute!" She grabbed for the box, but Mom held it out of her reach.

"Settle down, Teddy Jo. You don't have to carry on this way. You will like it here. You've got a little boyfriend. You won't be lonely."

Teddy Jo sucked in her breath and glared at Mom. Anger rose inside her until she thought her head would burst into a million, trillion pieces. She rushed at Mom and rammed her head right into Mom's stomach. Mom flew back and hit against the wall, then screamed and screamed.

Grandpa ran into the room, his face red, his hair awry. "Stop it, Carol!" He caught Teddy Jo's arm and held her firmly. She twisted and kicked and cursed loudly, but he hung on tightly.

"I'm leaving, Dad," said Carol, rubbing her stomach. "I'll call you when I can." She picked up Paul's box of clothes and comics and walked out of the room.

Teddy Jo stopped struggling and forced herself to go completely limp. Maybe she could catch Grandpa off guard and get away from him. But his grip on her arms stayed firm. She could smell the special smell of him and for just a minute she wanted to lean against him and sob.

"You and I will be just fine, Teddy Jo," he said quietly.

She gritted her teeth and narrowed her eyes and stood very still. She heard Mom walk down the stairs and call Paul. A door slammed. A car engine started. Her heartbeat roared in her ears and she couldn't hear anything else.

"Let's clean up this room," said Grandpa softly. "We'll wash Paul's sheet and blanket and air this room out so you can sleep nice and peaceful tonight."

She bit her tongue and kept her eyes glued to the threadbare carpet.

He slowly released her and stepped away from her.

She finally looked up at the big, broad man. "I hate you," she whispered hoarsely. "I'll hate you for as long as I live."

He shook his head and tears sparkled in his eyes. "No, Teddy Jo. You are going to learn to love. You're going to be free to love me and your parents and everyone around you."

She just stared at him. He was crazy if he thought that. She sank down on the edge of her bed and sat with her head in her hands.

6
The Plan

Teddy Jo leaned carefully back against the trunk of the large oak and let her legs dangle down on either side of the fat branch. This was her special hiding place. She'd found it the day after Mom and Paul left and she often sat there and thought about how it would be to be rich so that Dad wouldn't have to worry about unemployment and Mom could stay home and cook and do things with them the way Mark Allen's mom did.

Teddy Jo sighed and peeked through the branches to where Grandpa stood talking with two men. She couldn't hear what they were saying but they'd been there before and Grandpa had said that they wanted to log out his black walnut trees. He'd said no and Teddy Jo knew he'd be saying no again. Those trees were special to Grandpa for some strange reason and he wouldn't let anyone cut them down.

"I'd cut them down myself if I could," she muttered as she narrowed her blue eyes and tightened her lips.

A dog barked and she knew it wasn't the sharp yip-yip of Chainsaw. Besides, today Mark and Chainsaw had gone away with Mrs. Allen to visit Mark's grandma.

Mark was kind of nice. He didn't get mad when she got more property and money than he did in Monopoly. And he let her pet Chainsaw any time she wanted to.

A bee buzzed around her foot and she sat very still until it flew away.

Several minutes later she heard voices near her tree. She scowled. Had Grandpa discovered her hiding place? She peeked down and saw the two men who had been talking to Grandpa. Grandpa wasn't with them.

"We could do it easy enough, Bruce."

"You're crazy, Lyle."

Teddy Jo held her breath and watched as they stopped almost under her. What if they looked up? Would they be able to see her feet dangling down? Did the leaves cover her completely?

Bruce took off his cap and scratched his sandy hair. "We need these trees. There's a fortune here and that old man just sits on it."

Lyle chuckled and the sound of it sent a shiver down Teddy Jo's back. "It would take us an afternoon in here with our rig and we could have these trees down and gone. I heard he's going to be gone next Wednesday. We could do it then."

"But he'd know it was us!"

"How could he know, Bruce?" snapped Lyle. "He might suspect but what could he prove? Let's get to town and set it up with Martin."

"The neighbors would know something fishy was going on if they saw us here," said Bruce sharply. "They'd call the cops and we'd be caught red-handed."

"I'll forge a contract and what can they say? Besides, if we come in here like we're supposed to be here, nobody will question us."

"It sure would mean a lot of money for the company. We need those trees. If we can set it up, then I'll go along with it."

"Sure you will." Lyle clapped Bruce on the back and they walked out of Teddy Jo's sight.

She licked her dry lips with the tip of her pink tongue. Her heart beat so loudly that she thought they could hear it even while they walked away.

Had she really heard right? Were they going to cut down Grandpa's precious black walnut trees? Were they really going to steal them?

She leaned her head back and smiled a slow, secret smile. They were planning to do just that. And it served Grandpa right! He'd be the one to throw a fit and scream and cry and curse.

She frowned. Grandpa didn't swear ever. He

never said bad words and he never lost his temper.

But this time he would.

Teddy Jo grinned, then carefully climbed down the branches and dropped to the ground. She knew a terrible secret and she wouldn't tell it even if someone twisted both her arms or poured big black ants on her. It was a terrible secret, the best in the whole world!

A warm wind ruffled her tangled hair as she looked around at the tall black walnut trees. Why did Grandpa care about these dumb old trees? What kind of fortune was in them?

She darted from tree to tree, touching the rough bark, looking up at the small dark green leaves. Her heart beat faster and faster and her mouth turned cotton-dry. Finally she leaned against a tree, her head down, her pulse beating rapidly. Her red shorts and white tee shirt clung to her damp, hot body.

Grandpa would be sorry that he'd forced her to stay with him. He d be very sorry that he kept her from running after Mom and forcing her to take her along.

"Teddy Jo!"

She lifted her head, her eyes wide. She saw Grandpa standing near the shed, looking for her as he called her.

"Teddy Jo, come here!"

She swallowed hard. She'd go to him, but

she sure wouldn't tell him about the men who were coming to steal his precious black walnut trees next Wednesday.

"I'm here, Grandpa," she called, waving. He turned and saw her and waved back and smiled and she thought she was going to be sick.

She ran to his side and stopped beside him and he smiled. He smelled like peppermint from the breath mint that she knew he was sucking. She pushed her ragged hair away from her sweating face and stared up at him without smiling, without giving away the secret.

"Let's go for a walk, Teddy Bear Jo."

"Don't call me that!"

He winked at her and she scowled harder. "Everybody needs a special pet name. You're a special girl and I love you."

A tight band seemed to squeeze her heart and she stared down at the grass. "Don't start that dumb talk again."

He walked toward a tall maple and she followed. Today he wore dark green pants with a matching short-sleeved shirt. He stopped under the maple and looked up and she did too.

"See that branch, Teddy Jo?"

"I'd have to be blind not to see it!"

Suddenly he leaned down and kissed her cheek. She jumped back and rubbed it gingerly and he only smiled.

"What about the dumb branch?" she finally asked. She could still feel the kiss on her cheek.

"Your mom had a tire swing in this tree on that branch when she was your age and younger. She spent hours out here swinging on it."

Teddy Jo stared up at the branch and tried to picture Mom swinging on a tire swing, but she couldn't.

"When we get back from our walk, I'll hook up a swing for you, Teddy Jo."

She bit the inside of her bottom lip to keep from gasping aloud. She couldn't imagine a swing built special just for her. Did he think a dumb old tire swing would make up for him keeping her here?

"I've got an old tire in the garage that would work just fine." Grandpa shook his gray head with a wide smile. "I should've done that while Paul was here so he could've had fun on it, too." He shrugged. "Well, it'll be here when Paul comes for a visit. But for now you can enjoy it." He squeezed her thin shoulder and she jerked away from him.

"I don't care about any old tire swing." Just the thought of swinging high in the sky made her heart leap with excitement.

"I'm going to make a tire swing for you and that's that." He smiled, then walked toward the black walnut trees. "Your great-grandpa planted all those trees over there." He waved his hand and she looked at the large trees with a secret little smile. "And I planted these when I was no more than six years old."

She stumbled over a branch, then caught herself.

Finally he stopped beside a grove of trees that were no bigger around than his wrist. He smiled down at Teddy Jo and his blue eyes were soft and full of love. "You helped me plant these when you were here last."

She gasped. "I did?"

"Yes. You were a tiny little mite, only three years old, and you stuck the seedling in the hole I dug. Your hands got dirty and you sometimes stuck two seedlings in one hole, but you loved every minute of it."

She clenched and unclenched her fists as she looked around at the trees. A strange little warm feeling curled around her heart.

"These are for your future, Teddy Bear Jo."

She looked and looked at the trees. How could these trees be for her future? What did that mean?

Grandpa jingled the change in his pocket and a fly buzzed around his head. "My dad said that he planted trees for my future. When he planted all those black walnut trees folks said he was crazy, but he said there would come a time when the wood would be scarce from all the lumber mills and all the furniture companies cutting down the trees. And he was right, Teddy Jo. Once trees covered all this

51

land." He waved his hand and she looked and she couldn't imagine how it would look to have trees everywhere. "And then folks started cutting them down or having them logged out. Now, look around and you'll see places with no trees. But we have trees. We have black walnut and maple and oak and sassafras. In the fall I'm going to plant more black walnut seedlings and they will be for Paul's future."

Teddy Jo frowned. "How can trees help Paul's future?" To her Paul would always be the sad little boy with wet pants.

Grandpa rubbed his face and looked thoughtful. "He will always know that he has money if he needs it."

Teddy Jo looked at the trees again. How could trees be money? "I wish Mom and Dad had trees for their future."

"But your mom does! Look over there. I planted those for her when she was newborn."

"If they are money for her, then why does she have to work hard? Why does Dad worry about money? Why can't we all live together in a nice house and have nice things? Trees can't mean money or Mom wouldn't cry because she doesn't have money for food and rent."

Grandpa stiffened beside her. He looked down at Teddy Jo with a sober expression and cleared his throat. "You make a lot of sense, little girl. You sure do."

Teddy Jo looked up at Grandpa just as he wiped a tear from his eye. Why was he crying?

"When is the future, Teddy Jo? When is it time to take care of the present? I have been blind. But no longer!" He strode toward the house, his head up.

Teddy Jo had to run to keep up with him. What was he talking about? It didn't make any sense to her.

In the yard he suddenly turned to her and laughed a great shouting laugh and swung her high in his arms. He hugged her close and kissed her cheek; then he stood her up on the ground and hurried to the house.

She swallowed hard while she rubbed his kiss away. For one wild minute she wanted to run after him and grab his hand and have him call her Teddy Bear Jo. But she forced herself to stand in the yard with the summer sun beating down on her head. She didn't really want him hugging her or kissing her. And she sure didn't want him to call her Teddy Bear Jo.

7

Tire Swing

Teddy Jo stood in the shade of the large maple and watched Grandpa try to toss a long rope over a high branch. The rope jerked, then tumbled down around Grandpa's feet. He just picked it up and tried again, and he whistled happily as he did it. Teddy Jo shook her head in wonder. Why didn't Grandpa get impatient and angry and just leave the rope? And why was he acting as if he had a wonderful secret that was almost bursting out of him?

He'd stayed in the house a long time and then finally walked out as if he was walking on air. He had said, "Are you ready for your tire swing? I'm ready to make it." His blue eyes had twinkled and they still twinkled even after three tries at tossing the rope over the branch.

"Don't give up, Teddy Jo." Grandpa winked at her as he looped the rope around and around on his arm. "This time it'll go over. You watch and see. The others were just practice shots. This one's for real." He laughed and winked again and Teddy Jo bit her tongue to keep from laughing with him.

She rubbed her sweaty hands down her red shorts and waited, holding her breath, as he pitched the rope up, up to the branch. It flipped right over the branch and jerked and bobbed, then settled down where Grandpa could reach it. He passed his end of the rope through the loop on the other end and pulled. It knotted up at the branch and Grandpa laughed in delight.

"I told you, didn't I? This swing of yours will be ready in the shake of a lamb's tail."

Teddy Jo laughed, then quickly covered it with a loud cough. Her heart seemed to jerk and bob just as the rope had and her fingers itched to curl around the heavy rope. What would it feel like to swing on a tire swing?

Grandpa looped the free end of the rope around the tire and held it up. "Give me a hand, Teddy Bear Jo."

She hesitated, then held the tire in place while he looped the rope again, then tied a knot. Was this just another dream, or did she really have her very own tire swing?

Grandpa stood back and studied the rope and the tire. He pushed his fingers through his gray hair, then nodded and grinned. "Give it a try, Teddy Jo. I want to make sure the knot holds."

Her stomach knotted tighter than the rope and she rubbed her hands down her shorts. Finally she caught hold of the rope and scrambled into the tire. Grandpa gave her a gentle push and she tightened her hold.

"That'll be just fine," he said proudly. He swung her again, higher and higher, and a laugh popped out before she could stop it.

Much later Grandpa walked around to work in the part of his garage that he called his wood shop and Teddy Jo sat in the tire, gently moving back and forth. This was the best swing in the whole world. Nobody had a better one. When Paul came she'd share it with him and he wouldn't be able to believe that anything could be so much fun.

She looked across the yard and the black walnut trees seemed to jump into sharp focus. A bitter taste filled her mouth and she moaned. Once Grandpa learned how rotten she was, he'd kick her out and she'd never see him or the tire swing again.

Wasn't that what she wanted? She gritted her teeth and nodded. Of course it was!

She dropped out of the tire and walked listlessly around the sunny yard. She stopped at the pen and watched the fawn that Grandpa was soon going to set free. It would run into the woods and join other whitetail deer.

But what would she do when *she* was free of Grandpa? She twisted a piece of hair around and around her finger. She'd go home again, wherever home was now, and she'd share a room with Linda and smell Paul and listen to Mom and Dad fight.

She kicked into the grass with a scowl. Anything would be better than being here. Hot tears stung her blue eyes and she blinked them quickly away. She was no baby.

An old pickup rattled past on the road and she sneezed from the dust it raised. At the sharp yap-yap of Chainsaw she spun around to find Mark Allen walking toward her with the little black dog at his heels.

She waited until he was beside her. "I thought you went to visit your grandma."

"We just got back." He smiled and his dark eyes twinkled happily. His curly brown hair was cut short and showed off his ears that stuck out a little from his head. He was dressed in faded jeans and an orange and white tank top. "What'd you do today without me?"

She shrugged. She couldn't tell him that she'd sat in her special tree and overheard two men planning to steal Grandpa's precious black walnut trees. She spied the tire swing, and pointed to it. Mark turned and shouted happily.

He ran across the yard and Teddy Jo followed. Chainsaw barked excitedly. Mark grabbed the rope of the tire swing in a flying leap that sent it sailing into the air as he wrapped his legs around the tire.

"Yahoo! Yahoo!" he shouted as he rocked it wildly, one hand gripping the rope and the other swinging out over his shoulder and head.

Teddy Jo clapped her hand to her mouth and stared in fear. He was going to fall right off the tire swing, splat on the ground. How could he act so crazy?

After a long time he jumped off the tire. His face was red and his hair damp with perspiration. "You try it, Teddy Jo."

"Me?" She jumped back and shook her head. She could never run and grab the rope, then ride the tire like a bucking horse in a rodeo.

"Are you scared?" asked Mark in surprise. "You won't fall off if you hang on tight to the rope."

How dare he think she was afraid? She walked back away from the tire, then took a running start. She jumped and grabbed the rope, but she couldn't catch the tire with her legs, and it jerked hard. Pain shot through her arms and she let go of the rope and dropped to the ground. She turned on Mark, her eyes dark with anger. "You knew that would happen to me! You wanted my arms to jerk right off my body!"

He laughed, doubling over with his laughter, and she leaped on him, screaming at him. He fell to the ground and she fell

on top of him, swinging wildly with her fists.
He twisted away, then pinned her shoulders
to the ground with strong hands and sat astride
her twisting body.

"What's got into you, Teddy Jo?" he asked
sharply.

Finally she lay quiet and glared up at him.
"You wanted to hurt me, didn't you? You
like laughing at me when I'm dying."

He shook his head, but he didn't release her.
"I'm sorry I laughed. But you looked so
funny. You should've seen your face."

"Let me up!" She twisted and turned and he
finally released her. She jumped to her feet,
her fists doubled at her sides, and he slowly
stood up, staring at her questioningly.

"Why are you mad?" he asked with a slight
frown.

"I almost killed myself on that dumb swing!"

He shook his head. "No, you didn't. I've
missed lots of times and jerked my arms hard
like that. I never got killed."

The anger drained from her and she didn't
know what to say. She twisted her toe in
the grass and looked down at Mark's tennis
shoes.

"I'll teach you how to jump on the tire," he
said in a soft voice.

She nibbled her bottom lip, then finally
looked at him. "And you won't laugh?"

"I might. But you can laugh at me when I
look funny."

That was new to her and she thought about it awhile. Chainsaw rubbed against her ankle, then settled down at her feet with his chin on her left foot. "All right. Show me how, Mark."

He smiled and a warmth spread over her. She wanted him to keep smiling at her and never get mad.

"Maybe you should learn how to leap on the tire while it's not moving," he said. He caught the rope and jumped, and he straddled the tire and looked down at her with a laugh. "Just pretend it's a horse."

She nodded. She'd never ridden a horse, so how could she know how to get up on its back? But Mark didn't have to know that. "Do it again and then I think I can," she said.

By the time she learned, she was hot and sweaty and her dark hair was wet on her neck. She flew through the air and wanted to shout the way Mark had, but she couldn't.

Finally she slid down to the grass and her legs felt like rubber. She sighed in satisfaction as she walked out of the way of the swing, then sank to the grass. Chainsaw immediately rested his chin on her leg and fell asleep as Mark sailed through the air on the tire. She rubbed Chainsaw's back as she watched Mark. Her heart leaped for joy and she laughed, then closed her mouth and sat very still, her eyes wide in surprise at her happiness.

Just then Grandpa walked around the garage and Teddy Jo wanted to rush to him and throw her arms around him, but she sat on the ground with Chainsaw until that ridiculous feeling was gone.

Mark jumped off the tire. "Hi, Grandpa. I like Teddy Jo's swing."

Teddy Jo's swing. Oh, but that sounded grand coming from Mark.

"I'm glad you kids are having fun with it," said Grandpa. "How about going in with me for a dish of ice cream?"

Teddy Jo slowly stood up and walked with Mark and Grandpa to the kitchen. She started to wash her hands, then ran instead to the bathroom. She washed her face and hands, then brushed her tangled hair that hadn't been brushed for two days. She looked in the mirror, then looked closer. Were those sparkling blue eyes hers? Finally she shrugged. So, what did it matter if she was happy once in a while? It didn't mean a thing.

She hurried to the kitchen to have ice cream with Mark and Grandpa.

8

The Storm

Teddy Jo shivered even in the oppressive heat as she looked at Grandpa's wide back. She had to tell him about the bad men who were going to steal his trees. But how could she? She'd kept the secret this long and now it was only three days before Wednesday. How could she explain that to Grandpa?

He opened the gate to the small pen and the fawn ran to him. "This is the day, gal," said Grandpa as he walked the fawn outside the pen into the yard. "You're free."

Tears stung Teddy Jo's eyes and she wanted to push the fawn back inside the pen and lock the gate. It wouldn't be the same without the fawn to feed every day. She wrung her hands which hadn't had a chance to get dirty since Sunday dinner. "Grandpa, can't we keep her a little longer?"

"No, Teddy Jo." Grandpa shook his gray

head and tears sparkled in his eyes. "I wish we could for our sakes, but for this little gal's sake we have to set her free." He rested his big rough hand on the fawn's head. "She can't be dependent on us to survive, or she'll die first time she goes to the woods to live."

"But we could take care of her for always!" Teddy Jo swallowed hard as she stared up at Grandpa pleadingly.

"She wouldn't be happy to stay here always. And the law wouldn't allow us to keep her. She wants to be a free doe the way God created her."

Teddy Jo wrapped her arms around the fawn's neck and pressed her face against the dusty, rough neck.

"She'll stay around here for a few more days, Teddy Jo. You'll be able to say goodbye slowly." Grandpa squeezed her shoulder and she wanted to release the fawn and fling herself against Grandpa and cry until the ache inside was gone.

Teddy Jo turned away from the fawn and away from Grandpa and looked toward the woods. The ache increased at the sight of the black walnut trees and she quickly turned toward the tire swing. She pushed her damp hair away from her hot face. Any minute she knew she would shatter into a million pieces. Where could she hide to get away from everything, even from herself?

"Let's go inside where it's cooler," said

Grandpa. His blue shirt was wet at his armpits and down his back.

Teddy Jo suddenly felt very tired and listless and could barely pick her feet up to walk. She wanted to sink down on the grass and just lie there. A fly clung to her arm and she slowly brushed it away.

Grandpa opened the back door, then turned and pushed the fawn back so it wouldn't follow them inside.

Teddy Jo turned on the faucet and filled a glass with cold water. She drank thirstily, then wiped the back of her hand across her mouth. The hum of the refrigerator sounded loud and the smell of tuna fish hung in the air. Grandpa had said it was too hot to cook a meal, so they had tuna sandwiches and vanilla ice cream.

"Shall we try a game of chess?" asked Grandpa as he filled a glass with cold water for himself. "Mark probably won't come over in this heat. They have air-conditioning."

"We should go to Mark's house." Teddy Jo held her hair off her wet neck. She should've put it in ponytails as Grandpa had suggested, but she'd been too stubborn to do anything that he said.

She sank down on the couch and turned her head so the fan would blow right in her face. The loud whirr of the fan shut off any other sound.

Grandpa walked to his bedroom, then came

back wearing a sleeveless white undershirt with his blue pants. "That's better," he said as he sat in his rocker. "We might be in for a storm if this heat doesn't let up. You afraid of storms, Teddy Jo?"

Her stomach tightened. "No!" She frowned and looked down at her hands that clasped her knee. She sure wouldn't tell him that she hated storms especially if there was thunder and lightning. He didn't really care anyway. He was only asking for something to say. Grown-ups always did that. Before Grandpa could say anything more to her, she turned on the TV loud enough so she could hear it over the sound of the fan. She clicked the channels, then finally settled on Channel 8. She'd seen the movie before where Glenn Ford worked in an old circus, but she kind of liked it so she curled up in the corner of the couch and watched it again. She peeked at Grandpa to find him with his head back and his mouth partly open, snoring softly. Maybe she should turn down the TV so he could sleep better. But she sat very still and watched him sleep with his arms folded across his broad chest. Part of his arms was deeply tanned and part was white.

A lion roared on the TV and she jumped and turned back to watch.

Maybe when Grandpa woke up she'd tell him about the bad men who were going to steal

the black walnut trees. Even if he hated her
for keeping it a secret this long, she'd tell
him. And he would find a way to stop them.

She tugged on the neck of her tee shirt. How
could she tell Grandpa? And why should
she? If she wasn't careful she'd be wanting to
stay here with him and she'd soon be sitting
on his lap and giving him hugs and kisses like
TV kids did to their grandpas.

He smacked his lips and snored a little
louder and she jumped in alarm, then settled
back in her corner and forced herself to
watch TV.

A small box with a "W" in it appeared in the
corner of the TV screen and fear pricked
her skin. She knew it was a weather warning
and that meant a storm.

"Wake up, Grandpa!"

He jerked forward. "What? What?"

"There's going to be a storm." She frowned
at him.

He read the list of counties that moved
across the bottom of the TV screen. "You're
right, Teddy Jo." He wiped his hand across his
face and blinked and cleared his throat. "But
we don't have to be afraid. God is our pro-
tection."

She frowned more and locked her clammy
hands together. God sure wasn't her protec-
tion. He didn't even know her.

Grandpa pushed himself up and walked to

the bathroom and she glared after him, hating him for daring to leave her alone for even a minute.

At bedtime Teddy Jo stood at the bottom of the narrow stairs and looked up uncertainly. She didn't want to sleep upstairs alone during a storm, but she sure wouldn't say anything to Grandpa. He'd walked around all evening as if nothing unusual was going to happen.

She rubbed her damp palms down her shorts and swallowed hard, then put one foot on the bottom step.

"Teddy Jo."

She turned quickly, her pale face lifted.

"I think it's too hot upstairs for you. Get your nighty on and bring a sheet and your pillow and sleep on the couch."

"I don't care if it's hot. I'm no baby."

"I know you're not." He smiled from where he sat in his rocker reading his Bible. "But I want you to sleep down here so that you'll be able to get some rest. I know how hot it gets up there."

She sighed and lifted her thin shoulders. "If I have to." She walked up the steep, narrow steps, her hand on the wall. In her room she grabbed her top sheet and pillow, then her nighty. She'd change in the bathroom. Thunder rumbled in the distance and she dashed for the stairs, almost falling over the trailing sheet.

She dropped the things on the couch and dashed to the bathroom. Her heart raced and she almost dropped her toothbrush when thunder rumbled again. If she was home right now she'd be huddled under the covers next to Linda.

Finally she walked out of the bathroom in her faded yellow nighty that just touched her bony knees. Grandpa had already made up the couch for her. She forced herself to walk instead of run to it.

"The weather will be cooler after the storm," said Grandpa as he stood his shoes neatly side by side near the kitchen door. He opened a drawer under the bookcase and pulled something out. He walked to Teddy Jo with a wide smile. "I just remembered this. Your mother used to sleep with it." He held out a small red and white dog with floppy ears.

Teddy Jo just stared at the stuffed animal, then finally reached out and took it. Part of its fur was rubbed off and part of it was still soft and fuzzy. She held it and looked at it and tried to think of Mom holding it and sleeping with it. She couldn't imagine Mom with a stuffed dog.

"Sleep tight, Teddy Jo. I'll see you in the morning."

"Good night," she mumbled. She watched Grandpa walk to his room and close the door behind him, then she hugged the dog to her.

It smelled dusty. She closed her eyes and listened to the whirr of the fan and finally drifted off to sleep.

Thunder boomed and she sat bolt upright, a scream caught in her throat. The fan was off and the room was inky black. Lightning flashed and the room lit up momentarily. Thunder boomed again and the windows sounded as if they would burst. She screamed, then screamed again and clutched the little dog to her. Wind blew, shaking the house, and she screamed louder, hurting her throat.

"Teddy Jo, I'm coming," said Grandpa in the darkness. "I'm trying to find a flashlight. The electricity is off."

She trembled and tears streamed down her face.

Suddenly rain lashed against the house and lightning flashed brighter and thunder clapped louder. "Grandpa! Grandpa!" She wanted to run to him but she couldn't move.

"I'm coming, Teddy Jo." A light bobbed at Grandpa's door and he hurried to her, kicking the couch in his rush. "Ouch!"

"I'm scared, Grandpa," she wailed.

He sat beside her and pulled her close to his broad chest. She clung to him, her face pressed into his neck.

"You're safe, honey. Nothing's going to happen to you. God is with us."

She sniffed and her body shook. He rubbed her back with his big hand and talked softly, soothingly to her. Finally the tears stopped and he pushed a hanky into her hands. She dabbed at her eyes, but still he held her.

The small light in the bathroom flickered on and the fan turned a few turns, then stopped again. The wind rattled the windows and whistled around the corners of the house. Lightning lit up the room again and Teddy Jo pushed her face tightly against Grandpa's neck. She wanted to stay there forever where she felt safe and protected. She could hear Grandpa's steady heartbeat, then it was drowned out by the whirr of the fan. Slowly she lifted her face and saw the small light on in the bathroom. She rubbed her fist across her nose and squirmed restlessly on Grandpa's lap. He must really think of her as a baby.

"The storm is over, Teddy Jo," he said cheerfully. "The wind has died down and the rain stopped. See. Even the lightning is dimmer."

She looked toward the window and knew that the storm was over. She sighed and reluctantly climbed off Grandpa's lap. He opened the windows and cool air rushed in, pushing back the hot, muggy air.

"Go back to sleep, Teddy Jo," said Grandpa as he straightened her sheet and picked her pillow up off the floor and dropped it in place. "The storm is over."

She laid down and he pulled the sheet over her, then kissed her cheek. She wanted to slip her arms around his neck and kiss him, but she curled her hands into tight fists and lay very still.

He set the red and white dog near her arm, smiled down at her, and walked to his bedroom.

She hugged the dog close and held her breath until she heard his bedsprings creak. "Good night, Grandpa," she mouthed.

Finally she turned on her side and closed her eyes, the dog tight against her heart. "Oh, Grandpa. How can you be so good to me when I've been so bad to you?" she whispered brokenly.

9
Paul

Teddy Jo carefully rinsed the last plate, then set it in the dish drainer. She pulled out the stopper and the water circled and ran down the drain. She walked to the window as she dried her hands. When would Grandpa come in from working in his wood shop? She had to tell him about the bad men before she lost her courage. She bit her lower lip and stared out into the sunshiny day. She'd tried to tell him before breakfast, but he'd said that he had to finish a chair for Mrs. Weaver because she was coming to pick it up at eleven.

Teddy Jo walked to the dish drainer and carefully dried and put away the dishes. For sure she'd tell Grandpa about the bad men after Mrs. Weaver left. If Grandpa got mad and kicked her out, then let him. But she couldn't break his heart by letting someone steal his precious trees.

She frowned and balled up the dish towel. If Grandpa had been mean and nasty, she'd have kept the secret. Things sure weren't working out right.

After the kitchen work was finished, Teddy Jo walked slowly into the living room and clicked on the TV. She stood close to it and watched a game show that she hadn't seen before. She flipped to a different channel and watched a soap opera that Linda had watched for a while last summer. She clicked it again and watched a peanut butter commercial that made her hungry just for a minute. She hadn't been able to eat the eggs and potatoes that Grandpa had fried for her.

Impatiently she clicked off the TV and silence pressed in on her. She tugged her gold tee shirt over her dark blue shorts. She curled her toes in her sandals that were getting too small for her.

Slowly she walked to the couch and sat down. She listened for Grandpa, then when she didn't hear anything, she reached behind the throw pillow and pulled out the red and white dog. One eye was missing. She hugged him close and rocked gently back and forth.

Just then a door opened on the porch and she stuffed the dog under the pillow and jumped to her feet, her heart racing. She waited for the door to open and Grandpa to walk in. But he didn't walk in. He knocked and

she frowned. Why didn't he just walk in?
But maybe the door was locked.

She rushed to it and opened it wide, then
stumbled back with a gasp. Dad and Paul stood
there. She swallowed hard as she locked
her hands together behind her back.

"Where's Grandpa?" asked Larry as he
stepped inside and looked around.

"In the garage," said Teddy Jo barely above
a whisper. Why was Dad here? Had he come
to pick her up to take her back? But it wasn't
September yet.

Paul rushed to the bathroom and slammed
the door.

Teddy Jo stared at the closed door, then
back at Dad. He was dressed in faded jeans
and a sleeveless tee shirt with one pocket.
He looked so small after seeing Grandpa
all the time. He smelled like sour beer.

"I'm leaving Paul here. Linda can't manage
him. He's been taking after you, Teddy Jo."
Larry smiled but the smile didn't reach
his blue eyes. The dark smudges under his
eyes made him look very tired.

"I sure can't take care of Paul!" she said
sharply, gripping the arm of Grandpa's rocker.

"Grandpa can. At least for a while." Larry
rubbed his dark hair back and then let it
flop to his wide forehead again. "I'll go find
him. You see about Paul."

Teddy Jo stood very still while Dad walked
out of the house. She heard the toilet flush,

then a few minutes later Paul walked out with
his stained white tee shirt half in and half
out of his denim shorts that were too large on
his thin body. His feet were bare and he
looked pale and washed out, as if he hadn't had
any sun at all this summer.

"I'm staying here," said Paul with his chin
high and his eyes daring her to disagree.

"You sit right here and wait while I find
out what Grandpa says." Teddy Jo waited until
Paul sank to the couch, then she ran out.
The sun burned the top of her head and almost
blinded her.

She stopped just outside the garage and
caught her breath. She smoothed back her hair
and lifted her foot to take a step, then stopped.

"She's your responsibility, Larry," Grandpa
said gruffly. "You should be taking care of
your own children."

"I know Teddy Jo's a handful, but Paul
won't give you any trouble. It's just that his
sister can't manage him. She's only twelve."

"And why can't Carol take care of them, or
you?"

"We've both got jobs. We have to keep food
on the table. We've still got car payments
to make and the rent and just plain living. If
we weren't both working, we'd go under."
Larry's voice was angry and defensive.

"If you'd take my offer, it wouldn't be that
way." Grandpa for once sounded impatient.

"In twelve years we never asked you for

help, Ed Korman, and now when we do,
you complain. I told Carol you wouldn't want
Teddy Jo here with you, but she said you
did. If I could I'd take both the kids back with
me, but I can't. You're stuck with them
until September."

Teddy Jo stumbled back and quickly dashed
around to the back of the garage. She heard
Dad rush out, then roar out of the driveway,
gravel flying behind his tires.

She covered her hot face with trembling
hands and forced back the sick feeling.
Grandpa wanted to be rid of her! He had said
that he loved her but he'd lied for some
reason. Grandpa didn't want her or Paul. He
wanted them to go home with Dad.

From deep inside her, white hot anger rose
and Teddy Jo jumped to her feet and ran
into the house through the back door. She'd
get Paul and run away where no one could
find them.

Grandpa and Paul were talking in the living
room and Teddy Jo caught herself back. She
couldn't stand the sight of Grandpa right now.
She looked wildly around the room, her chest
rising and falling.

She spied the large glass vase that Grandpa
prized above all else in the kitchen. Mom
had bought that for him. Teddy Jo trembled
and the vase swam before her eyes. Oh, she
hated Mom and Grandpa and Dad and
everyone!

She climbed up on a chair and lifted the vase off the shelf. She stood quietly on the chair, the vase in her hands. She remembered Mom and Grandpa talking about it, telling what it meant to them.

She lifted the vase high above her head.

"You can break it, Teddy Jo, but it will hurt you more than me," Grandpa said in a quiet voice.

She glared at him. "I hate you!"

"I'm sorry that you do. I love you."

"You don't! You don't! You don't want me or Paul. You didn't really want the little fawn. You don't want anything but your dumb old trees. And you won't have those for long!"

Grandpa rubbed a large hand over his face. "Teddy Jo. My little Teddy Bear Jo. What has made you so angry? Did just seeing your dad do this to you?"

She shivered and almost lost her balance. Grandpa reached for her but she screamed, "Don't touch me! I hate you!"

"You get down from that chair this minute, young lady!" His voice boomed out at her and she almost fell off in her surprise. "Set that vase on the table and get off that chair now!"

She stared at him, her mouth gaping open in surprise.

Grandpa stood with his feet apart, his hands on his hips and his eyes like steel.

Teddy Jo trembled as she stood the vase on the table next to the salt and pepper shakers,

then slowly she stepped to the floor. Her
legs felt like hot plastic.

"Now, sit down and tell me why you are this
upset."

She slid onto a chair and watched with wide
blue eyes as he sat across from her.

"Start talking, Teddy Jo. Now!" Grandpa
locked his fingers together on top of the table.

She swallowed hard and twisted a strand
of dark hair around her finger. "You don't want
me. You don't love me."

"I want you and I love you."

She shook her head hard. "I heard you
talking to Dad."

"Then you know what I said."

She nodded with a frown.

"So, you know why your dad was so angry
at me." Grandpa leaned back in his chair
with a tired sigh. "I didn't want you to know."

She gasped and held her stomach, fighting
against the searing pain inside. He was
admitting that he didn't love her after all, that
he didn't even want her. Oh, but she was
glad she hadn't told him about the trees. Let
him lose his precious trees. Then he'd know
the pain she was feeling right now. And he
deserved all the pain possible. She slowly stood
up. "I'll help Paul take his things upstairs."

"He can sleep across the hall from you."

She shook her head. "He can sleep in the
same bed as before in the room with me. I can
take care of him that way."

"You don't have to take care of him. I will."
Grandpa tucked his shirt in better, then
jangled his change.

She lifted her chin and looked him right in
the eye. "You don't have to take care of me or
Paul. I will. You take care of your trees and
leave us alone."

He frowned at her as she sailed past him to
find Paul. He was curled up on the couch
watching a game show on TV with his thumb in
his mouth and the little red and white dog
held against his heart.

"We'll take your box of stuff upstairs, Paul,"
said Teddy Jo as she picked up his box. "I'll
find some shorts that fit you better."

He pushed himself off the couch and rubbed
his wet thumb down his stained shirt. He
looked ready to cry. "They hate me. Linda beat
me and always left me alone when she went
off with a boy."

"You'll like it here. You can swing on my
tire swing." She walked up the steep stairs and
he followed. She set his box at the foot of
his bed, then rummaged through until she
found a pair of tan shorts that would fit him
better. She pulled out his worn tennis shoes
and he put them on. She tied them because
his knots were too loose to stay for long.

"Grandpa's nice," he said in a low voice.

She shook her head hard. "No! He acts
like it, but he's not. And don't you forget it."

Hot tears stung her eyes. She'd better not forget it either.

Flies buzzed at the window. A dog barked outdoors and she knew it was Chainsaw. Today she didn't want to see Mark or his dog. If they came over, she'd send them packing.

"Can we go swing now, Teddy Jo?"

"Sure. Come on." She took a deep breath and walked with Paul down the steep stairs, through the hot house that smelled like cabbage, and outdoors.

Paul touched the tire swing, his eyes wide.

"I'll show you how to get on," she said without a smile.

Would she ever be happy again?

10

A Shared Secret

Teddy Jo swung her legs over the side of the bed and peered into the darkness. What was the strange noise? A gentle breeze blew in the window and the nightlight in the hall kept back total blackness.

She walked slowly to Paul's bed. She could smell his dirty tennis shoes as she stopped at the side of his bed. She leaned close and her heart dropped in alarm. Paul wasn't in his bed. But maybe he'd gone down to the bathroom without waking her up to go with him as they'd agreed on before he'd finally fallen asleep. He probably woke up and wanted to prove to her that he was no baby, so had walked downstairs alone.

She turned to her own bed, then heard the strange noise again. A shiver ran down her spine and she rubbed her hands down her cotton nighty.

She walked slowly to the doorway and looked down the short hall to the steps. Had the sound come from downstairs? She cocked her head and listened again. The sound was coming from the other bedroom! Had Paul lost his way and ended up in the wrong room? Or had some stranger walked into the house and up to the bedroom to find something to steal?

Teddy Jo trembled, then squared her shoulders and lifted her chin. She would march right into the bedroom and find out who was in there. No strange noise would keep her from looking.

At the bedroom door she stopped and licked her dry lips. Someone was in there! She could hear breathing and a sniffing sound and she wanted to race downstairs for Grandpa.

Her hand trembled as she reached for the light switch. She clicked it on and blinked against the brightness, then gasped as a white blob sat up in the bed. Her eyes widened in fear and she clutched the sides of the doorframe. Then the sheet was pulled aside and Paul sat in the middle of the bed, blinking in surprise. His eyes were red and his face wet with tears. He looked at her a long time, then flipped over and buried his face in the pillow and his thin body shook with sobs.

She stood in the doorway, her heart thudding painfully, tears blurring her vision. The strange noise had been Paul's sobbing.

Should she call Grandpa to take care of him?

She shook her head hard, then roughly pushed her tangled hair out of her face. What did Grandpa care?

A cricket chirped and other night noises drifted through the open window.

Teddy Jo clicked off the light, then slowly walked to the bed and sat on the edge of it. The springs creaked. Paul's sobs continued.

Finally she crawled across the big bed and lay close to Paul and put her arm around him with her head close to his. He snuggled against her and she blinked hard to keep her tears from falling.

He stopped crying and lay still beside her. She didn't know what to do. In the past when Paul had cried in the night, she'd let him cry.

He sniffed hard and turned and touched her face. "I lied about Linda," he whispered brokenly.

Teddy Jo blinked in surprise.

"I did. I said she was mean to me and that she always left me alone, but she didn't. I just wanted to come back here with you and Grandpa. I wanted to see the deer and pet Chainsaw and sit on Grandpa's lap."

"Oh. Oh, my."

"Don't hate me, Teddy Jo." He rubbed her cheek and it felt very strange to Teddy Jo to have her little brother touch her. "Don't tell Grandpa or he might send me back."

"You can stay here." She thought of her

terrible secret and what Grandpa would do
when he lost his trees and she trembled. After
that both she and Paul would be kicked
right out. But she couldn't tell Paul any of that.
She rubbed his back and felt his bones through
his skin.

"I wish Mom and Dad and Linda could come
here to live. But Dad says over his dead
body and Mom says she could arrange that."

Teddy Jo sighed. So, Paul did listen to the
arguments. She had thought that he'd learned
to shut everything out, but he'd only pre-
tended to.

"I told Grandpa to talk to them and tell them
to live here and he said he would."

"Don't count on it." She felt him stiffen.
"I mean, you know how stubborn Dad is.
Grandpa might not be able to talk him into it."

"He will. Grandpa can do anything." He
sounded proud and she closed her eyes tight,
wishing she didn't know how Grandpa really
felt about them.

"Go to sleep, Paul."

He sighed and curled tightly against her.
She tugged free enough to pull a blanket over
them, then held him close.

When she opened her eyes again the sun
was streaming into the room and Paul lay on
his back with one arm over his eyes and
the other one hanging over the edge of the bed.
She smiled and a strange tenderness filled
her. She wanted to protect and take care of

Paul. She wanted to make him happy.

She frowned. What could she do for him? She couldn't even help herself. And Grandpa wanted to be rid of them.

A dog barked outdoors and a car without a muffler drove past. A fly buzzed at the top of the window and the curtains fluttered in the morning breeze.

Slowly Teddy Jo slipped off the bed, then walked to her room and quickly dressed. She brushed her hair so hard, tears filled her eyes. Awkwardly she put her hair in two sloppy ponytails, then pushed her feet into her tennis shoes and tied them tightly. Tomorrow would be the end of their stay with Grandpa. A bitter taste filled her mouth.

Impatiently she walked downstairs and the smell of coffee filled the rooms. Was Grandpa still in the kitchen? But maybe he was outdoors walking through his precious trees, loving them and talking to them as if they were family.

She stopped in the kitchen doorway, her heart lurching at the sight of Grandpa sitting at the kitchen table, a mug of coffee in his large hands. He looked up and smiled and said, "Good morning, Teddy Jo. My, but you look pretty today."

She frowned. What other lies would he tell her today?

"Do you want bacon and eggs or cold cereal?"

She reached in the cupboard for a bowl. "I want Cheerios." She didn't want to talk to him or she might scream and yell and tell him all about the men coming to cut the trees—so that she could see the pain on his face.

Grandpa sipped his coffee, then set the cup near the empty plate with smeared egg yolk on it. "I made the final arrangements for the trees to be cut."

She plopped down the milk jug and milk popped up and out the top and down the sides onto the counter. How could he make arrangements for the trees to be cut? Did he learn about the bad men, then make some sort of agreement with them?

"You look surprised, Teddy Jo."

She licked her dry lips and nodded. "I didn't think you knew."

He frowned. "Why wouldn't I know?"

She shrugged helplessly as she gripped the milk jug handle tighter. Why wasn't he angry?

"It's about time I saw my mistake," he said, shaking his head. "You helped me realize how wrong I've been."

She walked to a chair and sank down before she fell down.

"I was hanging onto those black walnut trees for the future. Only the future never seemed to come. But your folks need money now. I made arrangements for the Yonkers Brothers Company to come Thursday to log out the trees that my dad planted. They're buying them for veneer to sell to furniture companies. And the money will buy a house for your family, Teddy Jo. It'll put food on your table."

She stared speechlessly at him. It had to be a dream.

"I've been trying to tell them about God's love for years now, but they wouldn't listen. All at once I realized that Jesus always showed his love. To a hungry man, a loaf of bread is showing love. To a sick man, healing is showing love. And to a poor man, meeting his needs is showing love." Grandpa rubbed his hand up and down his arm. "It's about time I started showing love. And I'm doing it by selling trees to give money to my family who needs it."

Teddy Jo felt as if her head was spinning around and around. Could Grandpa mean what he was saying? She cleared her throat. "I heard you tell Dad that you didn't want us." It was hard to talk around the lump in her throat.

"I said that your place was with them. Families shouldn't be split up. You need your mom and dad. Paul does too. I told your dad that I'd help him so that all of you could be together again. He doesn't want my help. But I'm going to do what I can anyway. And I want a happy family, not one torn apart the way it is now."

She could tell by his eyes that he was serious. He loved all of them. He loved her!

He wanted them to be happy. And she'd ruined it by keeping her mouth closed about the bad men.

She slipped off her chair and rushed out the back door and across the yard. Her heart felt ready to burst. What kind of girl was she? How could she be so mean? How could she hurt Grandpa? If she told him about the bad men, he'd hate her. And if she didn't, they'd steal the trees that Grandpa was planning on having cut Thursday for her family.

She ran and ran until she was past the black walnut trees and into the maples and oaks and other trees that belonged to Grandpa. She stumbled over a root and almost fell, then caught her balance against a rough trunk and ran on.

A pain stabbed her side and her eyes burned with unshed tears. A twig caught in her hair and she cried out in pain as she struggled to free it.

Finally she stopped and leaned against a young oak with her head down, her chest rising and falling. She swallowed and swallowed to relieve the dryness in her mouth.

A squirrel scolded overhead and something rustled the leaves near her feet. Damp tendrils of hair clung to her flushed face and neck.

What a terrible thing she'd done!

She sank weakly to the dried leaves on the ground. She pressed her legs to her body and wrapped her arms around her knees. Two

giant tears welled up in her eyes and slowly
spilled over to run down her hot cheeks.
She bent her head and scalding tears gushed
out, wetting her face.

A firm hand gripped her arm and she looked
up with a shriek, her heart pounding in alarm.

Mark's Help

Teddy Jo jumped up, her eyes flashing with anger. "Why did you come after me, Mark Allen? I don't want you near me!" Once he learned her terrible secret he wouldn't have anything to do with her.

Chainsaw nosed through the leaves and Mark stood in front of Teddy Jo with his hands on his hips. His dark hair was damp and tightly curled with perspiration. "What were you running away from? I called you and called you and you kept on running."

"Can't you tell that I want to be alone? Take your dumb dog and get away from me!" Her legs ached from running and from the many scratches from bushes and branches.

"I won't leave you, Teddy Jo. You'll get lost out here by yourself. Come home with me." He knocked a spider off his jeans. "Grandpa's worried about you."

She covered her ears with her hands and shook her head. "Go away!"

He jerked her hands down. "What's wrong with you? Why're you acting so crazy?"

She swung at him and he jumped back with a surprised cry. "I want to be alone!" she yelled around the hard lump in her throat. "Get away from me."

He shook his head and his dark eyes flashed. "You are going back with me. You're going to tell Grandpa that you're all right so that he won't worry about you."

Grandpa would feel even worse if she saw him face to face and told him what was going to happen tomorrow. She turned away from Mark, her head down. An ant crawled up her arm and she flicked it off with a shudder.

"Please, Teddy Jo, tell me why you're so upset," said Mark softly from just behind her.

She shook her head and her ponytails bobbed. If he didn't keep quiet she would burst into tears again. And there was no way she'd cry in front of Mark Allen and Chainsaw.

"Are you mad because you have to stay with Grandpa until school starts?"

"No," she whispered huskily.

"Are you mad because Paul's here and you have to share Grandpa with Paul?"

Why didn't Mark go away and leave her

alone? She took a deep breath and clenched her fists tightly. "It doesn't matter about Paul," she said impatiently. She remembered how strange it had felt to hold Paul and comfort him.

"Do you really hate Grandpa the way you say?" asked Mark in surprise as he stepped around to face her.

She flushed and then suddenly realized that she hadn't hated Grandpa for a long time now. She loved him! Oh, it was too awful to think. She loved him and she was going to ruin him. Tears filled her eyes again and she knew Mark had seen them. She rushed at him, plowing into him with her shoulder. He plopped to the ground and she leaped on him savagely. He must not know how she felt about Grandpa. He must not see her tears.

He ducked her flying fists and flipped her off him, then pinned her to the ground the way he had once before. He breathed hard and she saw blood running from his nose down his lip and chin. It dripped on her and she squirmed, but he was too strong for her.

"Now, tell me what is wrong, Teddy Jo Miller. Tell me right now!"

His eyes looked even darker and he didn't even bother to rub away the blood. She whimpered and turned her head and closed her eyes.

He shook her shoulders. "Tell me right now!

I know something made you feel so bad that you had to run away. What is it? Tell me and I'll do what I can to help."

She lay very still, then finally looked up at him. She swallowed hard and sniffed. "I'll tell you," she whispered in agony. "But you can't help at all."

He slowly released her and moved off her. He sat cross-legged and looked at her and she pushed herself up, sniffing and rubbing her eyes.

"It's so terrible, Mark!" She locked her fingers together tightly.

"What?" He leaned toward her earnestly, his dark brows raised.

"I was in my special tree and I heard two men planning to steal Grandpa's black walnut trees." She knuckled a tear away. "They said they could come in and cut them and haul them away while Grandpa's in town on Wednesday."

Mark whistled under his breath. "My dad said that happens a lot. He said those guys make a lot of money off the poor man who ends up with nothing."

"Oh, oh!" She rocked back and forth. "And Grandpa is planning to sell some trees so Mom and Dad will have some money. Now, he can't! Those bad men will steal them all."

Mark leaped up. "Oh, no they won't! We'll stop them! We'll tell Grandpa."

She grabbed his arm. "No! You can't tell him! He'll hate me!"

"He would never hate you, no matter what."

"He would! He would! I know it!" She gripped his arms tighter and stared with anguish into his face. "Promise you won't tell him."

Mark narrowed his eyes, then finally nodded. "I won't tell him if I can help it. We'll think of a way to stop those men, but if we can't, then we'll have to tell Grandpa. He can't lose the money that those trees will bring. My dad said those trees are worth a small fortune."

It seemed strange to her that trees could be worth money, but she knew it was true or Mark wouldn't say it, nor would Grandpa. "How can we stop those bad men?" She felt a glimmer of hope and looked at Mark intently, waiting for him to speak.

"I'll call the police. We know the sheriff. He'll come and protect the trees." Mark's eyes sparkled and Teddy Jo almost laughed in excitement. "We don't want just to *stop* those men this time. We want to stop them from robbing *others* of their trees." He motioned with his hand. "Come on. Let's get to the house and make our plans."

"Do you think the sheriff will believe you? You're only a little kid."

"He'll believe me. He knows I don't make up things." Mark whistled to Chainsaw and they walked through the woods and Teddy Jo was glad she wasn't alone or she would've gotten lost.

Just at the edge of the black walnut trees, Teddy Jo said, "Wait, Mark." He turned and waited and she swallowed hard. "Why are you helping me?"

He frowned, his head tipped. "What do you mean?"

"Why should you help me?"

He scratched his head. "Why shouldn't I?"

"Nobody ever bothers with me. Nobody cares if they help me or not. Why should you?"

He rubbed his face, then smiled. "I'm a Christian, Teddy Jo. I love Jesus and he wants me to love others and help them. I want to help you. I want to help Grandpa."

Fresh tears stung her eyes and she ducked her head. Could being a Christian, full of God's love, really make that much difference? Maybe being a Christian was a good thing, then, and not to be criticized the way Mom did.

"Let's hurry, Teddy Jo." Mark whistled to Chainsaw again and the small black dog yapped and ran to Mark's heel.

Teddy Jo walked slowly through the woods and looked up at the large black walnut trees standing tall and straight. She walked past the younger trees that had been planted especially for Mom and then past the ones that she'd helped Grandpa plant. Would she be able to watch these trees grow to big trees that someone would want?

She stopped just inside the yard and wanted to turn and run again when she saw Grandpa pushing Paul on the tire swing. She hesitated and Mark said to keep walking, so she forced her legs to obey.

Grandpa turned around and smiled, his blue eyes full of questions. "I'm glad you made it back all right. But I knew Mark and Chainsaw would know the way."

She cleared her throat. "I'm sorry, Grandpa. I . . . I just had to be alone awhile."

He gently touched her flushed cheek. "I love you, Teddy Bear Jo."

She rushed past him and into the house where she sagged against the counter at the sink.

"I told Grandpa we were going to my house and he said it was all right," said Mark softly.

She nodded, then filled a glass with cold water and drank thankfully. She offered Mark a glass and he drank. She watched him and she suddenly realized that she'd never even offered anyone a glass of water before. Maybe she wasn't so bad after all.

12
Wednesday

Mark stopped so abruptly inside his kitchen that Teddy Jo bumped into him. She peeked around to see Mrs. Allen look up from peeling apples for a pie.

"What are you children up to? You look like the cat that swallowed the canary, Mark." Mrs. Allen laughed but her dark eyes were watchful.

Teddy Jo pressed closer to Mark and he shrugged nonchalantly and said, "Is it all right if I use the phone in the front room?"

Mrs. Allen nodded. "But don't stay on long."

"I won't." Mark rushed to the front room and Teddy Jo followed him as closely as she could. Her heart raced wildly and she wondered if Mark was a little nervous too.

He fumbled with the phone book, then finally found the number for the sheriff's department. He cleared his throat and looked at Teddy Jo. Her legs suddenly gave way and she dropped onto the edge of the rose-colored couch, her hands locked tightly together.

He asked for Sheriff Mason and she thought she'd faint dead away. And when Mark said that he'd see him in about an hour, Teddy Jo leaned back weakly and closed her eyes and wished that she was on the other side of the world.

Mark hung up and dropped to the edge of a flowered chair. "Maybe I should tell Mom."

Teddy Jo sat up like a shot, her eyes wide. "No! Please, don't, Mark! I'll die if you do! She might tell Grandpa."

Mark sighed with a shrug. "We'll do it your way." He jumped up and his dark eyes flashed with excitement. "Sheriff Mason said he'd meet us just down the road so that we can talk privately. We'll walk down there and wait for him."

Teddy Jo wrung her hands. "I can't do it. I just can't!"

"You have to, Teddy Jo. We don't want those men to steal Grandpa's trees or anybody else's."

Her stomach cramped and a bitter taste filled her mouth. She looked hopelessly at Mark, then rushed to the bathroom. She would not be sick right on the Allens' plush carpet.

An hour later Teddy Jo stood beside Mark in the driveway of a deserted farm house.

He'd made Chainsaw stay home because he said he knew Sheriff Mason wouldn't want the dog in his car.

"I hope he believes us," said Teddy Jo as she watched the black and white car pull up beside them. She rubbed her hands down her shorts as she looked at the redheaded man sliding from the car. He was dressed in a two-tone brown shirt and pants with a gun on his narrow hips. He rubbed his red beard and smiled at them.

"What's the story, Mark?" he asked.

Mark motioned to Teddy Jo. "This is Teddy Jo Miller. She's Grandpa Korman's grand-daughter. She heard two men plotting to steal Grandpa's large black walnut trees."

Teddy Jo waited for the sheriff to laugh and push the story aside, but he looked intently down at her. He stood with one hand on the butt of his gun and the other hand at his side. His hazel eyes were very serious.

"Tell me about it, Teddy Jo," he said as he pulled a pad and pencil out of his pocket.

She licked her dry lips and watched a bluejay fly to a low branch near the police car. Finally she told all she could about the men and why she didn't want Grandpa to know. "Please stop them, Sheriff Mason! I don't want Grandpa to lose his precious trees!"

Sheriff Mason thoughtfully pushed the small notebook and pencil back into his shirt pocket. "Teddy Jo, the way I see it, you'll have to make a choice right now. In order for us to really catch the thieves red-handed we'll need your grandpa with us to prove that he didn't sign a contract with them. If you can't tell him so that he can be with us, then the men won't be able to take the trees—but we won't be able to prove that they were trying to steal them." He squatted down in front of her and was almost eye to eye with her. "You are a brave girl to tell me about this. You can tell your grandpa. I've known him well the past eight years that I've been sheriff, and I know that he'll be proud to think you could trust him enough to tell him what you overheard. Don't be afraid to tell him. But I can't make you. You must choose yourself what to do."

She twisted her toe in the gravel and ice settled around her heart. She couldn't tell Grandpa. But she had to. She could see that all right. She lifted her chin. "I'll tell Grandpa." If he hated her and kicked her out, then he would. She loved him and she had to do what was best for him. She couldn't think of herself now. My, but it was funny to think this way. Was she even the same Teddy Jo Miller that she had been a few weeks ago?

"I'll go with you to talk to him," said Sheriff Mason as he stood up. "Do you want me to?"

She knew she was being a coward, but she said, "Yes. You too, Mark." She just couldn't be alone with Grandpa now. Maybe he wouldn't yell at her and kick her out with others to witness it.

Her legs were almost too weak to carry her around back of Grandpa's house. She peeked at the sheriff and Mark and they both looked very determined.

"Want to swing, Teddy Jo?" called Paul from the tire swing.

"Not now," she said in an unsteady voice. She watched Grandpa walk from the shed toward them and she knew he was wondering about the sheriff.

"Hello, Ed," said Sheriff Mason, holding out his hand.

Grandpa clasped it firmly. "Hi, Tom. What brings you here to visit us today?"

Teddy Jo sank to the grass and Mark dropped down beside her as Sheriff Mason explained to Grandpa what had happened. Finally Grandpa turned to Teddy Jo with a sad look. She wanted to run for cover but she met his look without flinching.

"Honey. I'm so sorry that this had to happen to you. I'm sorry that you were involved with those bad men. I hope you haven't suffered too much. It's a terribly big secret for such a little girl to carry around."

She blinked in surprise. He wasn't angry! He felt bad for her! What kind of man was this?

Mark nudged her and mouthed, "I told you so."

105

Grandpa laughed and slapped Sheriff Mason on the back. "Those boys are in for one big surprise. Let's catch them so that they can never do this again!"

On Wednesday morning Grandpa drove out of his driveway toward town just as he'd planned to do. Teddy Jo and Paul stood with Mark inside his house and watched till he was out of sight.

Paul squeezed Teddy Jo's hand and laughed excitedly. She'd told him everything and he'd been excited about helping catch the bad men. "Let's go to our hiding place now," he said, jumping up and down. His shoelaces clicked on the kitchen floor and Teddy Jo quickly knelt and tied them tightly.

"We have to wait a few more minutes," she said, looking longingly at the back door.

Mark watched the clock in deep concentration. "Fifteen minutes and we'll meet the sheriff and his men in the woods behind the black walnut trees."

Teddy Jo shivered and stared at the clock with Paul pressed against her. Their breathing and the hum of the refrigerator was all she heard for a full minute. Then a truck drove past on the road in front of the house. Paul jumped and Mark laughed nervously. Teddy Jo tugged at the collar of her pink shirt, then noticed a white streak on it where she'd dropped toothpaste earlier. She scratched at it, but it didn't come off.

Was Grandpa climbing into the back seat of the sheriff's car right now so that he could ride back and hide with the sheriff and his men?

Several minutes later Teddy Jo sneaked through the trees with Mark and Paul. She stopped beside Grandpa and he smiled and she smiled. He winked and she ducked her head. Paul reached for her hand and she held his small hand firmly. She could feel the pulse in his thin wrist and she knew he was very excited. Could they hear her heart beating?

"Here they come," whispered the sheriff from his position behind a large maple. Mark stood beside him without Chainsaw, who would have barked a warning.

The heavy equipment stopped near a car and two large trucks that hauled logs. Teddy Jo shivered and looked up at Grandpa. His eyes were narrowed and he had a very determined look on his face. He shifted his position and Teddy Jo's heart dropped to her feet. What if he walked out and confronted the bad men and they hurt him before the sheriff could stop them?

But Grandpa stayed there and watched as one man with a red cap directed the driver of the large yellow machine that would top out the trees. Just as the machinery was in place, the sheriff sauntered from behind the tree toward the two men that Teddy Jo had overheard that day.

The roaring of the machine stopped and

Sheriff Mason said, "Hello. Could I see your contract for these trees?"

Lyle stepped forward with a wide smile. "Sure enough, Sheriff. I'm sure Bruce has it in the car."

Bruce shook his head and pulled off his cap and scratched his head. "I sure thought you had it, Lyle. I suppose I could drive to town to our office and get it, but it sure would be a waste of valuable time."

"These trees are ours, Sheriff," said Lyle sharply. "You're wasting our time. And time is money."

"I'll ask the owner for his contract," said the sheriff as he pushed his cap to the back of his head. His bright red head looked like a flag among the greens and browns of the woods.

Teddy Jo wanted to rush out and tell the men to stop lying, but she didn't move.

"Wait," said Lyle, then laughed and shook his head. "I believe I have that contract right here." He pushed his hand into his pocket and pulled out a paper. "It's a copy of it. Will that do, Sheriff?"

The sheriff reached for it and read it and then took off his cap and scratched his head. "Do you think you'll have the trees logged out today?"

Lyle nodded. "With this equipment we can do a woods of this size in a matter of hours."

"So you'd be all done and gone before Ed Korman got home." The sheriff folded the paper and handed it back to Lyle who took it and stuffed it in his pocket.

Teddy Jo could barely breathe. Paul whimpered and she frowned down at him.

"Sure. We'd be done. I'm trying to do the man a favor. He wouldn't want to be here to see his trees cut down. They have sentimental value to him."

"Maybe that's why he didn't want to sell," said Sheriff Mason sharply.

Grandpa stepped out and walked toward the men and they stared at him in surprise. "Hello, boys. I don't remember signing a paper for these trees for your company. I could have sworn that I signed with Yonkers Brothers."

Bruce swore and Lyle stared at Grandpa as if he was seeing a ghost. The other men started to leave but the sheriff's men stepped out and told them they were all under arrest.

Teddy Jo tugged at Paul and they ran to Grandpa's side. Paul slipped his hand in Grandpa's and Teddy Jo wanted to rush to his other side and hold that hand. But she stood still and watched the police lead the bad men away.

"Thank you, Teddy Jo," said Sheriff Mason as he held his hand out for her to shake. His large hand closed over hers and she felt ten feet tall.

She nodded and quickly pulled her hand back.

"I'm proud of you, Teddy Jo," said Grandpa, smiling down at her.

She ducked her head and flushed hotly.

"Tomorrow we'll watch these trees being logged out and we'll be happy about it," said Grandpa. He swung Paul to his shoulders and Paul squealed with pleasure.

Teddy Jo wanted to ride on those strong shoulders but she knew she was too old. She watched wistfully as Grandpa carried Paul and talked with Mark. Quietly she walked beside them with tears burning her eyes.

A strong hand grasped hers and Grandpa said, "Come on, Teddy Bear Jo. Let's get to the house and have a tall glass of iced tea."

"All right!" she cried, laughing up at him.

13
Teddy Jo's Family

Teddy Jo paced across the living room nervously, then stopped to look out the window. Mom had said when she called yesterday that they'd be here about noon. How could Paul sit quietly and watch Saturday cartoons when he knew Mom and Dad and Linda were coming to talk about their future?

Rain splattered on the window, and while she watched, it stopped and the sun peeked from behind a cloud and shone brightly. The good smells of meatloaf and cole slaw drifted from the kitchen where Grandpa was fixing dinner for the whole family.

Paul touched her hand and she turned to find him looking up at her with wide blue eyes in a pale face. "They won't take us home, will they? They won't make us leave here, will they?"

She shook her head. "I don't think so. They

111

don't want us until two more weeks when school starts."

"I won't go then." He folded his arms and stuck his chin out. "I will stay with Grandpa always."

"I'm glad you want to," said Grandpa from the doorway. "If my plan works you'll be close so that you can come over every day."

Teddy Jo's heart leaped. "Do you have a plan?"

He nodded and his blue eyes twinkled. "And I have a heavenly Father who is going to help with my plan. He loves all of us and he wants us to be happy."

Teddy Jo fingered the back of the chair near her. "He doesn't love a bad girl like me, Grandpa."

"He does, Teddy Jo. He loves you very much. He wants you to know it. He wants you to be his girl and he wants Paul to be his boy." Grandpa sat on the couch and Paul crawled onto his lap. "Come sit with us, Teddy Jo."

She hesitated, then sat beside him and she could smell the onion that he'd peeled for the meatloaf.

"God can't be near as nice as you, Grandpa," said Paul, rubbing Grandpa's arm.

Grandpa kissed Paul, then chuckled. "Thank you. But God is much nicer than me. He loves you more than I do, too. He wants you to be happier than I do. He can take better care of you than I can." He patted Teddy Jo's bare knee. "God loves us so much that he sent Jesus to make it possible for us to have fellowship with him, and to take away our sins and put new hearts in us."

"I need a new heart," burst out Teddy Jo before she knew she was going to say it. She flushed but Grandpa only nodded.

"Yes, you do, Teddy Jo. Once I was a very bad person and I didn't know Jesus. When I learned that he loved me and wanted to make me into a new man, I gave myself to him. The Bible says that when I did that God gave me a new heart and that I was a whole new person inside."

"I want that," whispered Teddy Jo before she lost her courage. "I don't like to be so terrible."

"And I don't like her to be either," said Paul.

"We'll pray," said Grandpa as he held Teddy Jo's hand in his. "Thank you, heavenly Father, for loving all of us. Thank you for making the Miller family a happy family who love you. And thank you that Teddy Jo wants to give herself to you. Forgive her sins and give her a new heart."

Teddy Jo listened to him pray and she silently prayed too. Finally she lifted her head and Grandpa smiled at her. "I belong to God now and I have a new heart. I am a new Teddy Jo Miller." She laughed aloud and Paul did too.

"You look the same to me," Paul said with a giggle.

"But she's not the same. The new Teddy Jo is a Christian now. Before long the whole family will be." Grandpa kissed Teddy Jo's cheek and she didn't jump away from him. He winked and she winked back.

A car door slammed and Teddy Jo's heart almost dropped to her feet. "They're here," she whispered, her eyes wide.

"Don't be upset," said Grandpa softly. "I've prayed for this day and it's going to be a good one. You'll see."

Paul clung to Grandpa's neck, but Grandpa finally pried him loose and walked to the door. Teddy Jo pushed herself up and followed him. He said it would be all right and he never lied. It *would* be all right.

Grandpa held the door wide and Dad, Mom, and Linda walked in. They didn't look at all happy and Teddy Jo wanted to run upstairs away from them.

"Dinner is almost ready," said Grandpa after everyone had said hello to everyone else. "Come in the kitchen and we'll eat as soon as we can put it on the table."

Linda looked around, then smiled. "I remember that rocking chair. I remember you rocked me to sleep, Grandpa."

He nodded and kissed her. "That I did. You were five years old and as cute as a button. You're still a mighty pretty girl."

"Thank you." She tugged her suntop to meet her yellow shorts.

Teddy Jo waited for the sharp jealousy to seize her, but nothing happened and she beamed with pleasure. "After dinner we'll go swing on the tire swing, Linda."

"And maybe Mark will come over and you can see Chainsaw," said Paul as he pushed past Linda to walk into the kitchen.

"I'll help dish up dinner," said Carol as she washed her hands at the kitchen sink.

Larry stood at the back door and looked out in the yard. Teddy Jo stood beside him. "See the tire swing, Dad? Did you ever have a tire swing?"

He looked down at her with a strange look on his face; then he smiled. "I had one when I was about your age. My brothers always beat me to it, but I did get to swing on it."

"You can swing on that swing," she said. "We'll take turns."

He looked at her, then at Grandpa. "Did you work a miracle, Ed?"

"God did." Grandpa set a bowl of mashed potatoes on the table with a pat of butter melting on top. "We'll talk more later. Larry, would you help Teddy Jo fill six glasses with cold water? There is nothing like a good glass of cold well water to go with a fine meal."

As they ate, Teddy Jo peeked at Mom every once in a while until finally Carol said sharply, "What is it, Teddy Jo?"

She swallowed hard and squirmed in her chair. "Mom, I'm sorry for hurting you when you were here last."

Carol blinked and flushed. She twisted her napkin. "I'm all right now. I hope it never happens again."

"It won't," said Teddy Jo firmly. She wanted to say more but she couldn't. A wave of love for her family washed over her and she felt overwhelmed. She didn't know that she loved her family.

Larry held his fork in mid-air. "What's new, Ed? How are the trees? Or shouldn't I bring that up?"

Grandpa chuckled and Paul laughed. "We have had a lot of excitement around here lately because of our black walnut trees. I'll tell you all about it, but first let me say that I've been wrong in my thinking. Those trees are for us now and not just for the future. What good are trees if you can't get some help out of them?"

"I've never heard you talk this way, Dad," said Carol in surprise.

Grandpa winked at Teddy Jo and she winked back. "Teddy Jo taught me a lot this summer."

"We like it here," said Paul, talking around a cucumber slice.

"I can see that," said Larry thoughtfully.

"This is a good place to raise kids," said Grandpa.

116

"No place is good if you don't have the money for it," snapped Larry. He reached for the plate of meatloaf, his brows almost meeting over his nose as he frowned. Teddy Jo wanted to take his hand and tell him everything would be all right if he'd just listen to Grandpa's plan. But would he?

The rest of the meal was quiet and then Carol said she'd do dishes if everyone would leave her alone in the kitchen.

"Come see the tire swing," said Paul as he tugged on Linda's hand.

Linda shrugged. "All right, but I don't know what the big deal is."

For just a minute Teddy Jo wanted to slap Linda the way she had in the past, but she pushed that bad feeling away and said, "Just wait and see. It's so much fun to swing on it."

"I'll bet." Linda flipped her dark hair over her slender shoulder and walked across the grass to the swing.

Just then the whitetail fawn walked into the yard and stood with its head up, watching them.

Linda gasped and Teddy Jo and Paul rushed to the fawn. Oh, but it was good to see it again!

Teddy Jo rubbed its neck and talked softly to it and Paul kissed its face.

"I never touched a deer before," said Linda in awe. She tentatively rested her hand on the deer's flank. "Oh, my. It's so cute!"

Teddy Jo told her about Grandpa taking care of sick or hurt animals until he could set them free again.

"I thought Mom and Dad said he's a weird old man," said Linda, looking toward the house.

"He's not!" cried Paul, his eyes flashing.

"I thought he was very strange at first," said Teddy Jo. "But then I saw that he was different because he loves people and things and he never gets mad or swears or anything."

"That's because he's a Christian," said Paul proudly. "So are me and Teddy Jo."

"And you both really like it here?" asked Linda with a puzzled frown.

"Yes," said Teddy Jo. "I'd hate to leave and so would Paul."

"Dad doesn't know I know it, but he got laid off again. And Mom's job pays so little that she wants to get a new one. She talked to him about living here and working in Grand Rapids."

Teddy Jo's heart leaped and she caught Linda's hand. "That would be great! I want them to stay here."

Linda tugged her hand free, then turned to look at the house. "We couldn't all fit in there. And they don't have any money left to rent a place. Dad said he might have to get food stamps again and whatever other help he can get from the government."

"Grandpa has a plan," said Teddy Jo. "He says he'll tell us all together today."

"What is it?" asked Linda sharply.

Teddy Jo shrugged. "I don't know, but it'll be good." She twirled around the yard, then plopped down on the grass. Oh, but she couldn't wait to hear Grandpa's plan!

14
The House in Middle Lake

Teddy Jo stopped in the kitchen for a glass of cold water. She smiled as Mom hung up her dish towel.

Carol studied Teddy Jo's face. "You seem like a different girl, Teddy Jo. It is amazing."

Teddy Jo licked her lips, then quietly told Mom what had happened to her and that now she was happy. "I hated myself before, Mom. I hated it when I got angry and had fits and broke things, but I couldn't stop myself."

Carol pulled Teddy Jo close for a minute, then released her. "I guess none of us have been happy, have we? You probably want to stay with Grandpa and never go home with us."

Teddy Jo looked down at the floor, then up at Mom. "I don't want to leave Grandpa *ever*."

"Paul feels the same way. He told me that he'd lied about Linda and that she took good care of him, but he wanted to be here. I wish there was a way for us to stay. It's so peaceful here. So quiet."

"I think you're right," said Larry from the doorway.

Teddy Jo stood very still and waited for the usual fighting, but Dad slipped an arm around Mom.

"I had forgotten what fresh air was like. I don't think I really like city life. Your dad said there's a factory in Grand Rapids that is hiring now. He said there's a good chance that we could both get in. And that would be very good pay."

Carol studied his face. "Are you serious, Larry?"

He nodded. "I'm tired of the life we lead. I'm tired of the fighting and the tears. I would like our family to be together and with both of us trying, maybe we can manage the kids." He looked at Teddy Jo. "I don't think we'll have any more trouble with her."

"You won't," she said quietly. She wanted to hug them both but she couldn't. Maybe someday she'd be able to hug and kiss as easily as Grandpa.

"I might take a loan from your dad if he's willing to give one," said Larry. "I hate to, but I don't see any other way right now."

Just then Grandpa walked in, smiling that secret smile that Teddy Jo had seen lately. "I want to take you all on a little ride," he said as he jingled his car keys. "I already sent Linda and Paul to the car."

"Where are we going?" asked Carol as she tucked her blouse into her slacks. "I should comb my hair and fix my makeup a little."

"It's not necessary," said Grandpa. "But if you want to, go ahead. We'll wait in the car for you."

Teddy Jo walked past Grandpa and he caught her and swung her up in his strong arms. She stiffened, then laughed and slowly slipped her arms around his neck. Her face burned and she pushed against him and said sharply, "Put me down."

He kissed her, then set her on the floor. "I'll race you to the car, Teddy Bear Jo."

She laughed and ran past him and out the door into the bright sunlight. A water puddle from the morning rain stood near the side of the car. Birds sang in the trees in the front yard. Teddy Jo felt as if she could fly.

She stopped at the car and turned and laughed gaily as Grandpa finally caught up with her. "I beat you, Grandpa."

"You sure did. I sometimes forget about these old legs." He opened the car door and she slipped into the back beside Linda and Paul.

Several minutes later Grandpa drove along a tree-lined street in Middle Lake, then parked on a paved driveway. "We are going

123

inside for a while," he said, motioning toward a brick house with natural wood trim.

"Who lives here?" asked Carol as she peered out the window.

"Let's go in," said Grandpa with another secret smile.

Teddy Jo felt like leaping and twirling, but she walked with the others up the walk to the front door. She waited for Grandpa to ring the doorbell, but instead he pulled a key out of his pocket and inserted it in the lock. He opened the door and they all walked in.

"What's going on, Ed?" asked Larry with a frown. "We can't just walk through this house."

"I have permission to show you through," Grandpa said with a twinkle in his eye. "See here. This is a fine living room with a brick fireplace."

"Where is the furniture?" asked Linda as she looked around.

"There isn't any right now," said Grandpa. He led them down a hall and showed them four bedrooms and two baths as well as a kitchen, dining area, and a full basement downstairs.

Teddy Jo watched a spider spin a web in a basement window. It was cool after the heat upstairs.

Finally Grandpa led them back to the living room. He sat on the raised hearth and looked at them and Teddy Jo felt little shivers of excitement run up and down her back. She rubbed her hands down her shorts, then locked her fingers together behind her back.

"Larry, Carol, and kids," said Grandpa softly. "This house is yours if you want it."

Carol gasped and Teddy Jo stared at Grandpa to see if he was teasing.

"How can that be?" asked Larry sharply.

"The money I got from the sale of the black walnut trees is for now, for all of you now. I always said it was for the future, but I was wrong. We can't just plan for the future and go without today. So, I sold the largest black walnut trees and with the money I'd like you to buy this house. You don't have to. You can take the money and buy a house anywhere you want, but I do want my family around me. I want Teddy Jo and Paul and Linda. And Carol I want you. And Larry. There's enough money to furnish it and to pay the taxes for a few years."

Carol burst into tears and buried her head in Larry's shoulder. He held her and Teddy Jo saw tears in his eyes.

"I can't let you do this, Ed," he said.

"Larry, the trees belong to all of us. I just had the say on cutting them down, and I never wanted to do it before this. I was wrong. I must make up for my past mistakes. And I need you here with me. I need to watch my grandchildren grow up. But if you want to live somewhere else, I'll just take the time from my woodshop to visit regularly." Grandpa pulled a big blue hanky out of his back pocket and blew his nose.

Teddy Jo held her breath and waited for Dad to say something. He just had to agree to living here.

Paul moved close to Teddy Jo and gripped her tee shirt and held it tightly.

She tried to smile reassuringly at him, but her face felt frozen.

"I am going to move in here to live," said Linda with a toss of her head. "I don't care what the rest of you do."

"It's for the family to decide, Linda," said Grandpa softly. "But I'm glad you vote yes."

"I vote yes," said Paul.

"Me, too," said Teddy Jo barely above a whisper.

Carol touched Larry's cheek. "Please, Larry. We could be happy here. And it's close enough to a city that we wouldn't feel out of everything. Please."

He waved his free arm. "When do we move in?"

Teddy Jo jumped up and down and shouted almost as loudly as Paul.

"You can sign the papers Monday and move in immediately," said Grandpa. You can get your furniture right away. The money is in the bank in an account for you both."

Carol walked slowly to Grandpa and she hesitated, then kissed him. "Thanks, Dad. Thanks."

"I love you, Carol," he said softly. "You are more important to me than all my black walnut trees."

She shook her head and tears flowed down her cheeks. "I never knew. I never knew."

Teddy Jo blinked hard to keep from crying. Slowly she walked down the hall and looked in each room. She stopped in one that had yellow walls with a gold carpet and she just stood there, looking around. This would be her bedroom. She looked up at the ceiling but there was no water spot in the shape of Michigan or any other state. So what? It was a great room anyway.

She turned at a step behind her to find Grandpa in the doorway. He smiled and said, "I thought you'd like this one the best."

She looked up at him and he seemed to fill the room. Suddenly she rushed to him and flung her arms around his waist. "Thank you, Grandpa! Thank you very much!"

"Thank you, Teddy Jo."

She looked up with her eyebrows raised questioningly. "For what?"

"For the hug."

She flushed and ducked her head, but kept her arms around him. "I guess it's time I treated you like a grandpa. I guess I could crawl on your lap and give you hugs and kisses."

"And that's a greater gift to me than anything that money could buy," he said huskily.

He knelt down and she touched his cheek with her finger tips. "You're my girl, Teddy Bear Jo, and don't you ever forget it."

"You're my grandpa." She kissed him on the cheek and she could smell his skin. She laughed and hugged him around the neck and kissed him again. Finally she stood back from him and looked at him with a smile. "I love you, Grandpa."

He shouted with laughter and swung her up into his strong arms, her feet dangling in mid-air. "Those words are worth more than gold, Teddy Jo."

"They are worth more than black walnut trees," she said.

He laughed with his head back and she threw her head back and laughed a great shout of a laugh just like his.